Ace

Cameron Hart

Published by Cameron Hart, 2024.

ACE

First edition. September 20, 2024.

Copyright © 2024 Cameron Hart.

ISBN: 979-8224574957

Written by Cameron Hart.

Want a free book?

Sign up for my newsletter[1] and get your free copy of Chasing Stacy!

One look at the stunning waitress carrying the weight of the world on her shoulders, and I'm a goner. I wasn't looking for a sweet little thing with auburn hair and more baggage than I can fit on the back of my bike, but there's no going back now. She's mine. I'll prove to her I'm more than capable of handling her past and making her feel safe again.

---

1. https://dl.bookfunnel.com/7wbqvhsx8r

Chapter 1

Lennox

"Twenty-ounce half-caf latte with light foam and sugar-free vanilla coming right up, Stella!" I smile at one of my favorite customers as I load up the espresso hopper and start assembling her drink.

"Bless you, child," the older woman says dramatically while stuffing a five-dollar bill in the tip jar. "I don't know how you manage to memorize everyone's order. I can barely remember to put my wig on most days."

I giggle at Stella as I steam the milk for her beverage. "I would never have guessed it wasn't natural."

Her boisterous laughter bounces off the walls of the coffee shop, causing a few of the other patrons to look up. Stella has bright purple hair today, the curls pinned in an elaborate updo with a pink bow on top, resting slightly off-center. Yesterday, her hair was teal. Last week, it was fire engine red.

"Don't you go telling anyone my secret," she says, tapping her nose.

I make the universal signal for zipping my lips shut, which only makes her laugh harder. It's no secret that Stella Arnold keeps the boutique wig shop down the street in business.

I pull two perfect espresso shots into the waiting cup, then pour the hot milk over the top, holding back most of the foam and watching the white and caramel brown colors mix together. Using a spoon, I scoop out a marshmallowy dollop of foam and place it right on top, completing Stella's order.

Her metal and beaded bracelets jingle as she reaches for the coffee, and she sighs in appreciation as she takes her first sip. "That's the good stuff right there," Stella says to no one in particular.

"We do our best here at The Grind."

"Thank dear sweet baby Jesus for that," she says, her words dripping with the southern drawl we're known for here in Tennessee. Stella takes another sip of her drink, then heads out the door, bracelets clanging and heels clicking as she goes.

She's always been a regular customer at the coffee shop, but she started her daily visits last year in a thinly veiled attempt to keep tabs on me after my aunt passed away. That's also when her five-dollar tips started. Stella's generosity has kept the lights on in my little studio apartment on more than one occasion, but she won't acknowledge that she's helping me out at all. Stubborn old woman.

I wipe down the counter and clean off the steam wand, prepping the espresso machine for the next order.

"Did I miss Stella?" my co-worker, Maribel, asks as she steps out of the back room with a stack of cups.

"She just left."

"What color was her hair today?"

"Purple with a pink bow."

"Classic," Maribel says with a smile as she restocks the to-go cups and lids. "I want to be like her when I grow up," she says wistfully.

"And when will that be?" I tease, tossing an espresso bean at her. It bounces off her forehead, making us laugh.

"Never, according to Racheal," she sighs. The mention of her boss at the newspaper causes her to deflate.

"Still no real assignments?" I ask, resting my hand on my friend's shoulder.

Maribel shakes her head. "I know I'm an intern fresh out of college, but how am I expected to learn anything or grow as a journalist if all I do is get coffee for people? That's what I do *here*!" She throws her hands up in frustration.

I lean against the counter, listening to my friend's struggle. "Maybe you could find your own story and cover it instead of waiting for Racheal's approval?"

"My own story," she repeats, tapping her pointer finger against her lips. It's one of Maribel's habits when she's thinking. She also likes to braid and unbraid her hair, but the long black locks are tied up in a messy bun today, thus limiting her options.

"Yeah, I'm sure this town is crawling with stories for you to report on," I continue as I refill the espresso hopper. "Like... coffee. Where do we get it? Is there an underground coffee crime syndicate? Is it like olive oil? Did you know the Italian mafia controls a huge portion of the olive oil industry worldwide? How crazy is that?"

Maribel giggles and I look over my shoulder at her. "Our coffee comes from the roasters down the street, and they get it fair trade from farmers in Ethiopia and Columbia. I may have already tried going down that route," she admits.

"Fine, so there's no coffee conspiracy, but what about..." I trail off, trying to think of another angle for my friend. "What if you did an in-depth profile on someone in the town?"

"Oooh! I love that idea. There's just one problem."

"What's that?"

"There's no one interesting here," she deadpans.

"I'll try not to take offense," I tell her with a pout.

Maribel laughs, then heads to the register to help the customer who just walked in.

We get lost in the flow of taking orders and making drinks. It's busy for a Thursday morning, but I don't mind. I like having something to focus on. It helps to distract from the loneliness gnawing at me day and night.

It's not so bad when I'm at work or out running errands, but as soon as I get home, I'm aware of how empty my place is. How empty my *life* is.

My Aunt Maddy, God rest her soul, was a bright, bubbly force to be reckoned with. Until cancer ate away at her, bit by bit, dimming her light and eventually snuffing it out completely. She was my only family—the only one who ever stuck around, that is.

I don't remember much of my life before being dropped off on Maddy's doorstep at five years old. All I know is that my aunt scooped me up in her arms and gave me my first hug. She promised to always love me and take care of me. For fifteen years, she did just that. And now... Well, now I have to carry on her legacy.

Maddy Rose was everyone's friend. She didn't have a mean or judgmental bone in her body. My aunt had her vices, to be sure, smoking a pack a day being one of them, but she was sweet, carefree, and willing to help anyone in need. I wasn't the only stray to be dropped off at her home over the years. She made sure to always have a spare bed and an extra meal.

I can't afford many extra meals, and I only have a futon in my studio apartment, but I've been trying to honor my aunt's memory by doing a random act of kindness once a day. It isn't much, but it makes me feel close to her in a way. Good karma and all that.

"My favorite barista," a familiar voice says, breaking into my thoughts. I look up from the drink I'm working on to see Charlie, an old acquaintance from high school.

"Hey, Charlie," I say with a smile.

He's always been nice, but lately, he seems to be popping up all over the place. I think it started as concern for me when Maddy passed, but after a whole year, it's getting a little suffocating.

Charlie frowns, his dark brows furrowing. His left eye twitches imperceptibly, his green irises flashing with annoyance. But then he blinks, changing his demeanor completely. A broad grin takes over his face, but it doesn't look quite right. "I've told you a dozen times now, you can call me Chuck. All of my friends do."

I nod, giving him another smile, but I don't say anything else.

"Come on, loosen up, babe. We've known each other since tenth grade." He winks at me, but there's a bite to his tone.

Spinning around, I grab a twelve-ounce to-go cup and fill it with dark roast, leaving an inch of room at the top for cream. With my back turned to Charlie, I'm finally able to take a breath. He's been so intense lately.

"That's more like it," he says when I hand him his coffee. "You remembered my order."

I nod, not bothering to tell him I remember pretty much everyone's order if they've been here more than twice.

Thankfully, Charlie gets a phone call and leaves without making me feel any more awkward. When we were in high school, he barely noticed me. None of the guys did, at least not *that* way. So why is he hanging around so often these days?

I wipe off the counter and wander into the back room, hoping to find some dishes or something else to do. We had a bit of a rush this morning, so there's a tub of saucers and mugs that need to be run through the dishwasher.

By the time the dishes are done, the closing shift people have arrived. Maribel and I clock out and say our goodbyes. I promise to call her later, and she promises to find someone interesting in town to do a profile on.

I make my way down the street toward my studio apartment, each step heavier than the last. I hate going home. I hate sitting in my dark, depressing little room by myself. I've tried making it warm and cozy, but there's only so much a strand of fairy lights and a garage sale painting can do.

I've been on a shoestring budget since my aunt died. She took out a second mortgage on her house to pay for the cancer treatments and then defaulted on the loan a few months later. Long story short, the bank took Maddy's home, *my* home, and everything in it. They barely left enough to cover the funeral expenses. Just like that, I lost an aunt, a home, and any semblance of comfort.

Leaves rustle in the cool wind, and a few birds chirp at the disturbance. It's a gorgeous autumn afternoon here in Haven,

Tennessee, but I can't shake the dark clouds from my mind. Which is why it's the perfect time to search for today's random act of kindness.

I don't have a plan for what it will be, so I have to be prepared for anything. I usually have a backpack with me stocked with baby wipes, a first aid kit, snacks, extra socks, and even cleaning supplies.

My eyes catch on a gleaming row of motorcycles parked outside Rosie's Diner. Well, all of them are gleaming except one. My eyes narrow in on the bike on the far left. Dried mud is caked on the front wheel, with a few splatters on the headlight and handlebars. I don't know much about bikes, but I know who these particular vehicles belong to. The Dirty Sinners.

Some people in town might shudder at the mention of the local biker club, but that's just silly. Maddy knew people in the MC, and they were the most loyal friends she ever had.

I smile, remembering how a few of the Dirty Sinners crashed Maddy's visitation. Half the town was mortified when three big, burly bikers showed up with beer and a pack of cigarettes, placing both next to her casket, but Maddy would have loved every second.

With that thought in mind, I cross the street to Rosie's Diner. I don't know much about motorcycles, but I can clean a dirty bike. It's the least I can do for Maddy's friends.

Digging through my backpack, I pull out a rag, some baby wipes, and a bottle of water. I kneel in front of the mud-caked bike and unscrew the water bottle lid. I'm about to wash off the grime from the front wheel when I notice the bike isn't black like I initially thought. Instead, the body of the powerful machine is the darkest navy blue I've ever seen, with a million brilliant blue sparkles shining like stars in the galaxy.

I'm so lost in the fascinating paint job that I barely hear the door to the diner open and close. Something in the back of my mind registers the sound of boots on gravel, but it's faint, already part of the background as I continue to study the beautiful bike. Who knew motorcycles could be so pretty?

Not until a wall of shadow passes over me do I realize I'm not alone. Blinking a few times, I look up... and up, up, up, until I'm staring at magically dark blue eyes, the same color as the bike.

"What the hell are you doing?"

Chapter 2

Bright golden eyes blink at me, hitting me square in the chest with their beauty. The air drains from my lungs, and my heart squeezes painfully before thundering to life.

The stunning creature kneeling in front of my bike tilts her head to the side, causing a few strands of her long dark hair to flutter around her shoulders. What color is it? Not quite brown, yet not red. Auburn? I don't fucking know, but I think it's my new favorite color.

What is wrong with me?

I clear my throat and straighten my back, puffing out my chest as my hands ball into fists at my sides. It's a familiar stance, one I often use as the enforcer for the Dirty Sinners. Every one of my muscles tenses as I loom over the woman on the ground, blood pulsing through my veins in time with my hammering heart.

The longer I stare at the woman, the harder it is to look away. Dark eyelashes frame her wide, round eyes, and her nose is turned up slightly at the end, making her look like a goddamn doll. She nibbles on her bottom lip, drawing my attention there.

Jesus, her full lips look so juicy, so damn tempting, I'm finding it hard to concentrate on anything else. Especially when her little pink tongue darts out to lick away the sting of her bite.

A snarl escapes from some primal place deep in my gut, making me sound like a rabid beast.

What in the actual fuck is happening to me right now?

I was enjoying a few beers with my MC brothers when I noticed someone getting awfully close to our bikes. When they kneeled in front of the row of bikes, I jumped out of my seat and stormed outside the diner, ready to rip apart whoever thought they could disrespect Dirty Sinner property.

But now...

I blink a few times, realizing the woman is talking. I watch her lips form words, though none of them register in my brain. When she tips the water bottle she's been clinging to, I snap out of whatever spell she's cast on me.

"...I swear I didn't mean any harm. I wanted to do something nice," she finishes.

"Nice?" I repeat, the word sounding awkward and clunky on my tongue.

The woman nods, causing more of her auburn hair to fall forward, covering part of her face. I get the insane urge to tuck the strands behind her ears so I can see more of her beauty. She stands to her full height, which is only a hair over five feet if I had to guess.

My eyes flit down her curvy frame, soaking up her generous breasts, wide hips, and thick, juicy thighs. Never thought I had a type, but I think I just found it.

"Yeah, I try to do a random act of kindness once a day, and today, I thought I'd clean off this dirty motorcycle." Her radiant eyes flash with panic, and she immediately follows up with, "No offense. The other bikes are all shiny, and this one..." She trails off, dipping her head and breaking eye contact with me.

Why can't I seem to take a full breath now her attention isn't on me? A low, rumbling grunt leaves my lips, causing the curvy woman to flinch.

I swear to God Almighty, my heart just broke in fucking two at the thought of this innocent creature being afraid of me, but I can't figure out why. It's my job to intimidate anyone who poses a threat to the club, which leaves little room for empathy.

But this woman isn't a threat, is she? "Why?" I growl.

Her shoulders tense at my tone, and I want to punch myself in the face for scaring her even more. I don't know how to be gentle, goddammit. And I don't want to know. But for this goddess, maybe...

"Why, what? Oh, why do the acts of kindness thing?"

Those ethereal eyes hit me once again, and a thread of possessiveness weaves through every cell in my body, wrapping around my spine and filling my lungs with such intensity I find it hard to breathe. What is it about those champagne-colored eyes that make me want to curl my hand around the back of her neck and pull her closer, closer, closer until our lips and bodies fuse?

"Yeah," I mumble, unsure what to do with these outrageous thoughts ricocheting around in my brain.

The woman smiles, her lips parting slightly to show me her pearly-white teeth. Her golden eyes glint with pure innocence as she launches into an explanation. I get the feeling my girl is never without words for long.

Shit. Not my girl. *Where the hell did that come from?*

"Well, I don't know if you've noticed, but lately, the world seems to be going off the rails," she starts. The left corner of my lip twitches. Am I trying to smile? When's the last time that happened? "It seems like everyone could use a little more kindness, you know? I may not be able to donate thousands of dollars to cancer research or solve climate change, but I can make a care package for a cancer patient and make sure to recycle. Oh, and I never use plastic straws. I try to avoid plastic altogether, but I can only do so much. It's in everything, I swear." She rolls her eyes in the most adorable way, like a pissed-off little kitten.

Fuck me, who is taking over my thoughts right now? *Adorable kitten?*

"Anyway," the bubbly, mysterious woman continues. "It only takes a little extra effort to make someone's day. Being nice is the least we can do for our fellow humans, right?"

If anyone else said that to me, I'd scoff and tell them they're stupid and blind if they can't see how fucked up the world is. No amount of *random acts of kindness* is going to balance the karmic scales.

Golden eyes peer up at me, shining with such life and genuine joy, I can't bring myself to say a disparaging word to her. Incredibly, I find

I want to protect that innocence. I want to make the world the kind of place this woman thinks it is instead of revealing the darkness I've seen. The darkness I've caused.

My hands are stained with the blood of my enemies. And my heart? The fucker is cold and impenetrable, a black, useless piece of coal buried in my chest where my conscience used to be. I thought my days of feeling anything at all were long gone. Until honey eyes cut through my bullshit and gave me a reason to give a fuck.

I still don't know what she's doing to me, but I can't seem to send her away. The thought of scaring her off makes me break out into a cold sweat.

I'm aware of the awkward silence I'm creating, but I don't know how to have a conversation. I need to say something to her. Actual words this time, not grunted responses.

"Shouldn't be messin' with bikes, good deeds or not," I mutter. What is wrong with me? I'm not winning any points by being an ass. Not that I'm trying to win points or anything. Shit, this girl has me all messed up.

"Why not?" she asks, curiosity sparkling in those damn mesmerizing eyes of hers.

"It's personal property. You wouldn't go washing a random car, right? The same goes for motorcycles."

Her cheeks turn the prettiest shade of pink, then deepen to red. Every single thing about this woman enthralls me, and I have no idea why.

"Well, actually..."

"You've already washed a car parked in a diner that didn't belong to you," I state, loving how her blush turns crimson. I notice for the first time that she's wearing a black t-shirt that says *Not today, Satan,* on the front. It's all I can do not to smile, which is a new sensation for me.

Despite her nerves, the woman squares her shoulders and tips her chin up, a mischievous glint in her eye. "It was four cars, thankyouverymuch, and they were parked in the Haven Library." She crosses her arms over her chest, pushing her mouth-watering breasts together.

I rip my eyes away from her chest, afraid of making my erection even more obvious. My dick hasn't risen to the occasion in... shit, five years? No, that can't be right. Closer to ten, if I had to guess. Never bothered me before, but now I have ten years of pent-up sexual frustration bearing down on me, all of it directed at the curvy woman standing a mere three feet away.

"Bikers are a different breed than people who ride around in cages."

"Cages?" Her brow furrows in confusion.

I want to reach out and smooth my thumb over her skin and ease away the tension. Fucking insane is what I am. "Cars," I clarify. "Most bikers won't be as... *nice* as I am."

A purely joyful sound leaves her lips like tinkling bells or some shit. It washes over me, soothing the ache in my chest and loosening something deep in my core.

"I wasn't aware you were being nice," she teases. "I'm Lennox, by the way."

Lennox. The name of my new obsession.

She holds out her hand for me to shake, and I stare at it. I shouldn't touch her. I can't. I don't know what will happen once I get my hands on her. At the same time, I don't have it in me to be more of an ass than I've already been. It's a weird feeling, but I don't have time to process it right now.

"Ace," I respond, wrapping my fingers around her hand.

So damn soft. Her creamy skin is a stark contrast to my weathered and worn hands, darkened from long days in the sun and rough to the touch.

"It's great to meet you, Mr. Ace," Lennox says, another adorable smile stretching across her face.

"Just Ace," I grunt, wincing at my still too-harsh tone.

I can't seem to let go of her hand now that it's in mine. It's taking a considerable effort not to pull her closer and get a taste of her smile for myself.

"Well, Just Ace, is there something else I can do for you today?"

My heart stutters in my chest at her words. Could she possibly be offering up her gorgeous fucking body? It's been a decade since I've indulged in anything close to a one-night stand, but for Lennox...

Once would never be enough.

The thought slams into my brain, completely blindsiding me and rattling a few things loose.

Lennox must realize how her question came across at the same time I do.

"Not like that... I wouldn't even know how to... oh, my god, just..."

She withdraws her hand from mine, sending a shudder down my spine and leaving me cold and empty without her touch.

Lennox buries her face in her hands, muttering something incoherent. I think she's saying mean things about herself, which doesn't sit right with me. Her stuttered words echo in my mind. *I wouldn't even know how to...*

Surely she doesn't mean she's a virgin. A knockout like her? But she's so young, so damn sweet and pure... would it be surprising to discover she's innocent in every way? Furthermore, why in the actual fuck does that make me want to strip her right this second and claim her once and for all?

"Come by Dirty Gears tomorrow," I tell her for some reason. "You know where that's at? The bike shop?"

Lennox still has her head in her hands but fans her fingers out, allowing me to see her golden eyes peeking through. She nods, then drops her hands before wrapping her arms around her waist.

"Yeah, I work close by, over at The Grind."

I nod, tucking that piece of information away in the back of my mind. "Great. You can help me change my tire. They have actual polish, too. Not just water." I glance at the forgotten water bottle on the ground, then back at Lennox.

What am I saying? Change my tire? I don't need new tires, and if I did, I'd let Crank work on it. He's been tinkering with bikes since he was a teen. He bought Dirty Gears from the previous owner, and now all the Dirty Sinners get their mechanic work done there.

"Really?" She looks excited and a little nervous, and damn if that doesn't make me want to kiss her even more.

I nod. "This time tomorrow work for you?"

"Yes!" Lennox nearly shouts. She claps a hand over her mouth, a blush creeping back into her cheeks. "Sorry," she mumbles before dropping her hand. "I'm looking forward to it. I don't know much about motorcycles, but this one is gorgeous." She waves her hand in front of my bike. "Did you know it's not black? It's dark blue!"

A strange thing happens. The corner of my lips twitch, then stretch into an honest-to-God smirk. She's too fuckin' cute for her own good. And mine. "Crank does amazing custom paint jobs."

"Oh, yeah. Duh. Of course, you know what color your bike is." Lennox smacks the palm of her hand on her forehead.

I reach out before I can think better of it, looping my fingers around her wrist and drawing it away from her face. "Don't hurt yourself." Is that my voice? Why does it sound like gravel?

Lennox giggles. Fucking giggles. I don't know what to do with all of her sweetness, but it's suddenly overwhelming.

"Thanks for your concern, but I've got a pretty thick skull," she teases.

I grunt, not liking her demeaning joke. Even if she's kidding, I can't stand her thinking bad things about herself. "Tomorrow then," I grunt as I start to back away. I shove my hands in my pockets to keep from reaching out again.

"Can't wait!" she calls back, waving enthusiastically.

I stumble a bit, then spin on my heel, booking it back inside Rosie's Diner.

"What the hell was *that* about?" Rock, the Dirty Sinners VP, asks.

"I wish I knew," I answer as I take my seat next to him.

But I do know. I feel it deep in my chest. *That* was the beginning of everything.

Chapter 3

I wipe my sweaty hands on my jeans and cross the street, heading toward Dirty Gears. I should have brought another outfit to change into after work so I don't smell like the coffee shop. I could have dressed up a little, put on a nice top or something.

While I love my *People said follow your dreams, so I went back to bed* shirt, it's not exactly helping with my overall lumpy shape. Not that it matters. Ace would never look at me like that. Why would he?

The man is a force of nature. Six and a half feet of solid muscle, dark blue eyes the color of the ocean in a storm, and a deep, raspy voice that shot through me and sparked every nerve ending to life the first time I heard it. His earthy, minty scent still lingers in my mind, driving me crazy.

And when he wrapped his massive hand around mine? Holy. Freaking. Crap.

His hand engulfed mine, the calluses tickling my skin and sending a shiver down my spine. An unfamiliar pressure blossomed in my core, making my thighs squeeze together. I've had a dull, throbbing ache there ever since, and I don't know what to do about it.

I'm not totally naive. Even if I have zero experience with guys, I know what lust feels like. Or I thought I did. I've had fleeting celebrity crushes and gawked over shirtless guys on magazine covers, but nothing has ever come close to the all-consuming pull toward Ace. My body has been buzzing since our exchange yesterday, my skin sensitive and tingling whenever I think about his strong hands roaming over my curves.

Ridiculous, I know. He's a freaking Viking god who rides a badass motorcycle, and I'm a chubby barista doing my best to leave the world a slightly better place than when I entered it. We're opposites in every way. Oh, and there's the fact that Ace is probably at least a decade older than me. If he knew the crazy thoughts and desires that have been tying my stomach in knots all night, he'd surely laugh in my face.

"Lennox! Did you just get off work?"

My shoulders stiffen when I hear Charlie's voice behind me. I'm less than a block away from Dirty Gears, and I have half a mind to run the rest of the way and pretend I didn't hear Charlie call my name. I can't bring myself to ignore him, however. I know what it's like to feel invisible, and it would kill me if I made someone else feel that way. Even Charlie.

"Hey," I say casually, looking over my shoulder. "Yup, just on my way to run an errand." I keep walking toward Dirty Gears, hoping he'll take the hint that I'm busy. No such luck. Charlie falls into step beside me, forcing me to look up at him.

"Slow down, babe. Why the rush?"

I recoil at his pet name for me. I'm not his babe. I'm not his *anything.*

"I'm not rushing. I have an appointment I need to keep." It's not a lie. I *do* need to see Ace, though maybe not strictly for tire-changing purposes.

I squeeze the strap of my backpack and pick up my pace, not wanting to spend any more time alone with Charlie. Even though we're out in public in broad daylight, I still get an icky feeling in the pit of my stomach. I don't know what he wants from me or why he keeps insisting we're friends. I wish we would go back to the days when he ignored me, like in high school.

"Hang on a second," Charlie clips out. He grabs my arm, halting my movements. I gasp as he spins me toward him, then I yank my arm out of his grip. "Whoa, chill out, Len. I just want to talk."

Ugh. *Len?* No one calls me that. Is he trying to make up new names for me now?

"I'm busy at the moment with my–"

"Errand," he finishes for me. "Yeah, I heard you the first time."

Great, so then why are you still here? Of course, I don't say that. It would be rude.

"Listen," he continues. "I'm worried about you working all the time. You work too much. If you were my girl–"

"I work a normal amount," I tell him, cutting off that sentence before he can finish it. I have to bite my lips to keep from grimacing at the thought of being Charlie's girl.

"Then you won't be too tired to let me take you to dinner," he answers with a smirk.

I hate that he thinks he's so smooth. I especially hate the cocky confidence in his green eyes, like he truly believes he's God's gift to women, and I should be grateful he's deigned to take me to dinner.

"Um... I..." Shoot. What do I say? I've never been asked out before. I never thought I'd be in the position to turn down a date. "I'm busy," I mutter, taking a few steps back.

"You're busy every single night this week? I thought you said you worked a normal amount," he scoffs, though that cocky grin never leaves his lips.

I narrow my eyes at Charlie, hating this interaction more and more with each passing second. "I'm just... I'm not... dating right now. Thanks for the offer, though," I finish lamely.

Charlie's eyes flash with annoyance, and he moves toward me with surprising speed. I back up further, rearing my head back as he approaches.

"I'm trying to take care of you," he whispers. "I'm being nice. Isn't that what you want? A nice guy?"

"I, um..." I swallow the lump in my throat, blinking back tears. Why won't he leave me alone? My heart is racing out of control, my shallow breaths making it hard to form words.

"Let me take you out. Show you a good time," he insists. He smiles at me, but it's not charming or reassuring. Charlie looks like a predator, a hungry monster looking to devour its prey. "I'll even buy you a dress if you want, so you don't have to keep wearing those lame t-shirts."

I blink a few times at his comment, the pit in my stomach threatening to swallow me whole. I shouldn't care what this dick thinks, but his words still sting.

Charlie reaches for me, his fingertips grazing my cheek. I jerk my head away and stumble backward. I brace myself to hit the pavement, but instead, I'm pressed against a wall. A second later, the now familiar earthy, minty scent fills my lungs, and Ace wraps an arm around my waist, pulling me closer to him. My back is flush with his front, and I lean into his strength. I can breathe now that Ace is here, knowing he'll protect me.

I have no reason to trust the biker I met a short twenty-four hours ago, but I feel safer around him than I ever have around Charlie.

"Take a fuckin' hint and back the hell off," Ace snarls, tightening his hold on me. He spreads his hand out over my stomach in a possessive way, and I won't lie; I love it.

Charlie puts his hands out in front of him, palms up, in a sign of surrender. He walks back a few steps, and the tension drains from my muscles the further away he gets.

"Chill, dude," Charlie says, trying to act cool and confident. He's failing epically, and I suppress a smirk.

He thinks he's hot shit, a cocky, confident alpha who can take whatever he wants. But seeing him next to Ace? There's no contest. My big, burly biker is a real alpha. He doesn't have to prove himself to anyone. His commanding presence and silent strength speak volumes.

"I was just offering to help—"

"She doesn't need your help," Ace barks, cutting him off. "She has me."

Oh, lordy. I know he's just being protective, but I can't help picturing what it would be like to belong to Ace. To be his woman, the only one he lets slip under the wall he built around his heart.

I stand up a little straighter, squaring my shoulders and crossing my arms over my chest. Ace grunts and squeezes me closer, close enough to feel his hard abs and chest pressed against my back.

He dips his head down so his lips barely graze my ear. A shiver runs down my spine, the ache between my thighs throbbing and growing more intense by the second.

"You okay, sweetness?" Ace asks softly. How is his voice that deep and rough while still comforting me?

I nod, still trembling against his solid, rock-hard body.

"Want me to break his nose?" Ace grunts.

I snort out a laugh, turning slightly in his arms so I can look at him over my shoulder. I'm struck with intense, midnight blue eyes peering into my depths. I have no clue what this man is doing to me or what he sees, but something inside me shifts. Like I'm making room for my protective beast in my heart.

Insane, I know. But when the gruff, growly biker lifts his lips in a lopsided grin, I feel myself falling for him. Not just falling; I'm tripping all over myself to get him to keep looking at me like that.

"Not today, but maybe another time," I whisper to Ace. He grunts and rolls his eyes, finally sighing in defeat.

I notice how he's never let me out of his embrace. He's kept an arm at me at all times, anchoring me to him.

Charlie clears his throat, breaking our moment. I whip my head in his direction, and he looks at me expectantly, like he wants me to defend him. Yeah, not happening, *Chuck.* When he realizes I'm not going to say anything, he glares at me, those green eyes narrowing into slits. He huffs a frustrated breath, then throws up his hands and turns around, stomping away as he shoves his hands in his pockets.

I deflate against Ace, knowing he'll support me. We stay frozen in place for a second, and I soak up all of Ace's attention, memorizing how it feels being held by him. I'm sure this is the closest I'm going to get to this powerful man, so I want to remember every second.

An errant thought rushes to the surface, allowing doubt and insecurity to flood my system. I tense in Ace's arms, then wriggle out of his embrace, turning to face him. Deep blue eyes capture mine, a kaleidoscope of emotions buried beneath the surface. Concern, anger, and something altogether primal.

"Am I like Charlie?" I whisper, unable to keep the thought to myself.

"That his name?" Ace grunts.

I nod before continuing. "He keeps saying he's being nice by offering to take me to dinner and hanging around the coffee shop, but he's not nice. He's suffocating. Am I... am I suffocating? Do you even want my help? Am I–"

Ace closes the distance between us, crowding my personal space. I don't back away this time. This man is nothing like Charlie. I want his closeness. I want to breathe him in and feel the heat of his touch.

The enigmatic man dips his head, ghosting his nose across my cheek, down my neck, and back up until his lips tickle the shell of my ear. I shiver and rest my hands on his chest, my knees suddenly weak.

I curl my fingers into his black t-shirt stretched over the taut muscles of his chest. Ace growls softly, the sound reverberating around him and hitting me like a tidal wave.

"You're nothing like him," Ace murmurs, his warm breath tickling my skin. "Your presence is very much wanted."

I nod and nibble on my bottom lip, a nervous habit I've had since childhood. Ace surprises me by gripping my chin between his thumb and forefinger, tipping it up, and gently pulling my lip free from my torture. He stares at my mouth, and I wonder if he wants to kiss me as much as I want to kiss him.

"So beautiful," he says softly. His voice is so quiet, I don't think he meant for me to hear it.

Ace leans forward, and I part my lips, ready for whatever this man is about to do. I'm swept up in his aura, his strength, his pure masculinity. My fists tighten in his shirt, and I pull him closer, the tension between us growing unbearable.

A door swings open, banging against the side of the building where we're standing. Ace jumps away from me, dropping his hands to his sides as he takes a few steps back. I sway on my feet but manage to steady myself before I melt into a puddle of lust.

I look to my right, realizing we're next to Dirty Gears. A swarm of bikers file out the door, each one shoving it open and banging it against the wall with a loud thump. I dart my eyes back to Ace, who's running a hand through his dirty blond hair.

Crap, I've made things awkward. He was trying to make me feel better after the whole Charlie incident. He wasn't about to kiss me. I made it up. A silly fantasy. In fact, I'm not even sure why I'm here. Clearly, there are more qualified people to help Ace change a tire.

"I should go," I blurt, backing away.

"Lennox, I'm sorry if I made you uncomfortable. I–"

"I don't think I'd be much help with your motorcycle," I ramble, not wanting his pity. He obviously regrets getting close to me, and I can't process how much that hurts right now. I need to go home and bury myself in a blanket cave for the rest of my life.

"Wait, I'm–"

"It's okay. I'm not uncomfortable. I just..." I don't have an excuse for my skittishness, but I don't bother making one up. Instead, I spin around and run in the opposite direction, needing to flee this embarrassing scene.

Ace calls my name, but he doesn't chase me. Part of me wishes he would, but another part of me is grateful. It's all too much, and I need some air. Plus, I'm being ridiculous. I'm all worked up over a man who now thinks I'm crazy as a loon.

I look over my shoulder one last time and see Ace standing there, staring at me with an unreadable expression.

What am I doing? What am I running from?

I have no idea, but I get the feeling this won't be the last I see of Ace.

Chapter 4

Ace

"What's with that look on your face?" Beast asks as he hands me a beer. I've been hanging out at Sinner's Pour House for the last hour, trying my damndest to forget about the curvy enchantress who ran away from me yesterday.

I take a swig, then set the bottle down on the solid oak bar top. "What do you mean?" I grunt at the bartender. I adjust my features into a scowl. From the smirk Beast is giving me, I don't think I pulled it off.

"That dopey smile. I didn't know you had dimples," he jokes.

"I don't," I mutter, wiping a hand over my mouth to block Beast's view.

"Who's smiling?" Reaper asks from behind me. He sidles up to the bar and orders a double shot of whiskey before turning to me. "Ah. Ace is smiling? What's gotten into you?"

"Nothing," I say with a shrug as I tip back my beer. The cool liquid goes down easy, and I buy myself a few seconds of peace before Reaper says what I know he's going to say.

"Doesn't look like nothing. Looks like love."

I scoff at him and take another drink. "Just because you found your old lady doesn't mean love is in the air for everyone."

"Maybe not, but it's about some woman, isn't it? Your cheesy ass smile."

"Lennox is not *some woman*," I growl before I can think better of it. Reaper grins at me, knowing he's won. Dammit. I sigh and drag a hand down my face, finishing off my beer before addressing Reaper. "I don't know a thing about her, so it doesn't matter."

"Tell that to your face," Beast butts in, offering me another beer.

"No thanks," I decline. "I'm about to hit the road."

"Off to see your girl?" Reaper asks.

"She's not my girl." Not yet, anyway. *Not ever*, I remind myself. I'd stain her pure beauty. Ravish her innocence.

There's no way she would be with a fuck-up like me. A street rat who found himself in juvie at fifteen years old. When I got out, the Dirty Sinners seemed like a logical next step. I had nothing and no one, but my brothers at the MC took me in and made me one of their own.

"Keep telling yourself that," Reaper says. He gives me a knowing look before knocking back his whiskey. "You never answered my question. Are you going to see her? Lennox, right?"

Even though I know Reaper is head-over-heels for his woman, Arabelle, I don't want Lennox's name on his lips. A snarl escapes from deep in my chest, and I glare at him.

Reaper chuckles, holding his hands up in surrender, though he never stops laughing. "I'll take that as a yes."

Truthfully, I was planning on hanging out here all night, drowning my thoughts in alcohol. I tossed and turned all night, waking up periodically covered in sweat from yet another dirty dream about my girl.

Shit. Not my girl.

I have to keep reminding myself. Especially since she sprinted off after our almost-kiss. I thought she was right there with me, the way her fingers curled into my shirt like she was as desperate for my touch as I was for hers. But then the guys came thundering out the back door, breaking the spell.

I didn't want our first kiss witnessed by twelve of my brothers. Lennox deserves better. I could have sworn she was about to let me kiss her. And fuck, I wanted to. Needed to. I wonder what her lips taste like, how her tongue feels tangled in mine.

Christ, I need to get it together.

"Go on, then," Beast grunts, pulling me back into the present. "I can't have you smiling around here. You'll freak out the other customers."

I glare at Beast, then at Reaper, who chuckles at me. I love my MC brothers. I'd take a bullet for any of them, and they'd do the same for me. That doesn't mean they don't annoy the shit out of me sometimes. Especially when they're right.

I can't stop smiling whenever I think about her auburn hair and otherworldly eyes, shining with gold and innocence. And those curves... Jesus. I'd like to wrap my hands around her generous hips, pull her against me and devour her pouty lips.

It's more than lust, though. Sure, it's been years since I've indulged in a casual hook-up, but I don't want that with Lennox. The thought of tossing her aside after sleeping with her makes me want to rip out my heart.

Fuck. This is getting out of control. I don't know what to do with these possessive thoughts and feelings. When I wasn't dreaming about sinking nine inches deep inside Lennox, I was dreaming about holding her. Cradling her against my chest and promising her things I never thought I was capable of. Love. Commitment. A family.

Never wanted any of that. Never thought I deserved it. I still don't, but if Lennox saw something in me, maybe I'm not so horrible. Maybe my heart isn't as dormant as I think it is. Maybe...

I find myself pulling into The Grind and parking my bike. How did I get here? I certainly didn't mean to drive straight to Lennox's place of work. Apparently, my bike knows me better than I do.

What if she's not working? What if she *is* working?

My feet don't seem to care that I'm spiraling. They simply move forward, carrying me inside the coffee shop.

It's relatively empty in here, which makes sense. It's close to closing time.

"Ace?" comes the sweetest voice I've ever heard.

"Yeah," I grunt before clearing my throat. What the hell is wrong with me? I sound like a Neanderthal, growling out one-word responses.

Lennox doesn't mind. She gifts me with the brightest smile I've ever seen. I don't think I've ever had this much attention, and certainly not in a positive way. But I can't deny the sparkle in her beautiful golden eyes. She's looking at me like I'm the best thing in the world, and I don't know how to handle it.

I walk up to the counter, my heart beating out of my chest the longer I look at her. I flex my hands before balling them into fists at my sides. The urge to reach across the counter and pull her into my arms is overwhelming. Lennox is potent. Her presence is intoxicating, and I don't think I ever want to leave.

"You're here," she squeaks, her cheeks turning pink.

God, I want to nibble on them and kiss away her embarrassment. "I am." *Great response, idiot.* "Um, can I get..." I look over the menu hanging above Lennox, but it's all gibberish to me. "Coffee?" I ask, feeling foolish.

"Of course. Light or dark roast?"

"Dealer's choice," I say with what I hope is a smile.

Lennox goes to work filling up a mug with coffee. She doesn't leave any room for cream, which is perfect. I wonder how she knew.

"That'll be two dollars," she says as she sets the cup on the counter in front of me.

I hand her a twenty and tell her to keep the change. Those amber eyes widen in shock, and I can tell she's about to protest the large tip.

"It's the least I can do for making you uncomfortable yesterday," I cut her off before she can speak, breaking eye contact. Why I brought that up, I have no idea. I guess I need to clear the air. It would kill me if she thought I was taking advantage of her.

"No, it wasn't... it's not that I was uncomfortable," Lennox whispers before nibbling her bottom lip. She sighs, and I look up at her, wanting to take away her distress somehow. "I, uh... I thought I was making it up."

Her voice is so soft, I have to lean in to hear her. My hand moves on its own, reaching out to tuck a few strands of her silky hair behind her ear. "What do you think you were making up?"

Lennox's breath catches in her throat, those golden eyes locking onto mine. She stares at me, doubt swimming in her big, beautiful eyes. I cup the side of her face, silently encouraging her to trust me.

"Um..." she whispers. "Our, uh, connection, I guess. I don't know. It's stupid, but I thought you were going to kiss me, and then you jumped away, and–"

I slip my fingers into her auburn locks, wrapping them around the back of her neck and pulling her forward. Fuck this counter in our way. I lean over the annoying cock block, pressing my lips to hers, cutting off whatever doubts she has about my intention.

Lennox freezes at first, and I panic. *Shit, did she not want this? Am I screwing this all up for a second time?*

But then the softest, sweetest moan falls from her lips, her hands crawling up my chest and fisting my shirt. She pulls me closer, but the damn counter is the way. I break our kiss, though I keep her close with a hand at the back of her neck.

I get the strangest urge to kiss her forehead. So, I do. Can't say I've ever been this gentle, this aware of someone's presence. Lennox is overwhelming in the best way possible.

I already know I'm fucked when it comes to this woman. I'm a selfish asshole for wanting more. Once she finds out about my criminal record and the life I lived before joining Dirty Sinners, there's no way an angel like her would sink to my level.

"Wow," Lennox murmurs, her breath tickling my lips. I lean back, giving her some room. She blinks at me with something close to awe in those golden eyes.

"Did that clear things up?" I ask, giving her what I hope is a playful smirk. Can't say I've ever felt playful in my whole damn life, but this woman is bringing out all sorts of unexpected emotions in me.

"Yeah," she says, still breathing heavily. "Can we do that again?"

"Fuck yes," I growl, hauling myself up and over the counter.

Lennox gasps and steps back, and I land on my feet, stalking toward her. There's no hesitation this time. When my mouth covers hers, Lennox opens up for me, allowing my tongue to slip between her lips.

I kiss her in long, drugging strokes of my tongue, feeling her passion and heat as she wiggles against me. Lennox loops her arms around my neck, standing on her tiptoes and pulling me down to her level. God, I forgot how short she is. Tiny and curvy and so fucking adorable it hurts.

My fingers slide down her sides until I dig them into her hips, hauling her closer. Her generous breasts press against the hard slats of my muscles, and I groan, thinking about having her under me.

Lennox breaks the kiss, but I'm not done with her yet. I trail my lips across her jaw and down her neck, licking, nibbling, and kissing every inch of skin along the way. My girl slumps against the counter, trying to catch her breath.

I'm about to dive in again, but Lennox holds out a hand, stopping me. "Wait," she says breathlessly. "I should lock up before... before we do anything else." Her cheeks burn bright red, and I know it's not just from our kiss.

I slip my hand around her waist, drawing her closer to me. She peers up at me with such trust and admiration. I don't deserve any of it, but I want to be the good guy for once. I want to be someone Lennox would be proud of.

"We can do whatever you want, angel," I murmur as I nuzzle into the side of her neck. She relaxes against me, melting into my embrace. "But yes, you need to lock up. Can't have anyone else seeing what's mine."

"Yours?" she whispers, tensing in my arms.

"Fuck, is that too much? Too soon?"

Lennox shakes her head no as a brilliant smile stretches across her face. "Not too much."

She pushes up on her toes so she can kiss my cheek. No one has ever been this sweet to me. Never thought I wanted that, but with Lennox? I'll take whatever she's willing to give.

The enchanting woman spins out of my arms and skips to the front door of the coffee shop. She locks the door and turns off the open sign before looking over her shoulder at me. That blush still stains her cheeks, but I think she's more excited than shy. I hope.

"Come here, beautiful," I rasp, holding out my hand. My girl turns on her heel and nearly sprints back to the counter, going around the side and jumping into my arms. I scoop her up, loving the way she giggles. Lennox takes the hint and wraps her legs around my waist. I squeeze her ass and thighs, holding her against me as I walk us further into the back, away from the windows.

Fuuuuuck, she feels good right here in my arms. Right where she belongs.

"Where are we–"

I cut her off by leaning her against the nearest wall and devouring her mouth. I can't wait for another taste. I set her down so I can squeeze and appreciate every inch of her with my hands. Lennox opens for me and sucks on my tongue, making me growl. My hands grasp the sides of her neck, my thumbs caressing her jawline as I tilt her head to the side to deepen our kiss.

It's a frantic, desperate kiss like we're long-lost lovers who've found each other after searching the entire universe. It's cheesy as fuck, but it's the truth. The fact that she wants this as much as I do is a major fucking turn-on.

When we finally break for air, I rest my forehead on hers. "Jesus, I can't get enough of you, Lennox."

"Mmhm..." she manages to say in between breaths.

I take her lips one more time, sweeping my tongue inside and gliding it along the roof of her mouth. She moans so sweetly, so softly for me. When I pull back, her eyes are clouded over with lust. Goddamn, my girl looks good like this.

"More," she whispers against my lips.

"Fuck," I growl, the strangled noise raspy with lust. "Can I taste you?"

"T-taste me?" Confusion settles over her features. She realizes what I mean a second later. Her eyes go wide, those golden depths filled with lust and a little hesitation.

"Do you trust me, angel?" I murmur against the shell of her ear. Lennox nods, but I need more. "Need your words. Tell me exactly what you want."

"I w-want..." she trails off, tipping her head back as I suck on a sensitive spot beneath her ear. "I want you to... l-lick me," she stammers.

I growl, then drag my tongue up her neck, nibbling her ear. Lennox giggles, twisting away from me.

"No, I mean..." she sighs, her cheeks burning bright red. "Um, maybe you could..." Lennox swivels her hips, rubbing her pussy against my hard as fuck cock.

"You want me to lick your pussy, beautiful?"

"Mmmm," she moans, closing her eyes and nodding.

"Want me to make you come on my tongue?"

"God, yes," she whimpers. "Please, please..."

I growl, taking her lips in a punishing kiss. I break it only to thumb the button on her jeans open and pull the material down and off her legs, along with her panties. In one swift move, she's naked from the waist down, and I'm kneeling before her. I don't give her time to doubt herself as I throw one of her legs over my shoulder and lick her slit from bottom to top, making her tremble in my hands.

"Goddamn," I groan, savoring the first taste of my woman.

I suck on every part of her perfect pussy, letting her juices drip down my chin. She's marking me with her flavor.

I lift her other leg to rest on my shoulder, opening her up even more for me. I pin her to the wall using my body, my hands on her hips. She grips my hair and pulls as I eat her to a drenching orgasm. Lennox bucks against my mouth, coming hard and fast.

I lick her through it, adding my finger into her dripping entrance.

"Jesus, so tight," I grit out, slowly working my thick digit in and out of her.

"Please, please... more..."

Her pained pleas only spur me on. I drop my finger from her tight hole and trade it for my tongue, fucking her this way until she trembles and comes again. I let go of her hip and bring one hand down on her ass, smacking her once, twice, three times, until she's squirting into my mouth with another release, giving me what I need.

I growl into her soaking cunt, her juices driving me to the point of madness. I want more, but I know she's spent.

"Ace, ohmygod, oh god...Ace," she breathes out as she comes down from her high.

Lennox sags against the wall, her body limp, eyes closed. I carefully set her legs back down and lean her against the wall for support while I stand up. I wrap my arms around her and kiss her velvety lips, letting her taste her release.

She breaks the kiss, gasping for air, while I continue to nibble down her neck. I can't get enough of her.

"I had no idea..." she breathes out, still panting from everything her curvy little body went through. "I've never..."

I lift my head from where I was kissing her shoulder and peer into those amber eyes. So damn trusting. I'll make sure she never regrets it.

"Am I the first person to touch you like this, angel?" I rasp. I had my suspicions, but fuck, I like hearing her say it.

"Yes," she whispers. "Is that... okay?"

"Okay?" I growl, trying to reign in the possessive thoughts racing through my brain. "It's perfect. You're perfect."

Lennox smiles at me like I'm her hero, her prince charming, her favorite person in the world. Guilt twists my stomach and burns like acid in my throat. I'm not a good man. She wouldn't look at me the same if she knew all the shit I've done.

I can't bring myself to tell her about my past, nor can I seem to let her go. Lennox is *mine*, goddamnit.

I hold her until she regains her strength, and then I help her get dressed. When she's all put back together, Lennox looks up at me through her long lashes, still flushed from her orgasms.

"Let's get you home," I whisper, leaning down to kiss her forehead.

"I just have to empty the coffee carafes and sweep. I did everything else already."

"I'll sweep. You take care of the coffee?"

"Really?"

"Yeah, of course," I say, giving her my best smile. It's rusty, but when she returns it, I know I must have done something right.

Fifteen minutes later, I'm walking Lennox out the back door and into the parking lot. My bike is the only vehicle in the lot, and I give Lennox a questioning look.

"Oh, I don't have a car. I usually walk or take the bus."

I growl, not liking the idea of my girl walking alone in the dark. Sure, this small Tennessee town doesn't see a lot of crime, but still. I've seen and experienced enough shit to be paranoid about a sweet, young woman out late at night.

"I'll give you a ride."

"Are you sure?"

I stop walking and turn toward Lennox, cupping her cheek in my hand. "It's my honor to make sure you get home safely." *My honor?* I don't have much of that left, but it's the damn truth. I want to protect Lennox and her light at all costs.

"Okay." She tries to hide her smile, but I see it all the same. She likes me taking care of her. Well, there's plenty more where that came from. I've never had these possessive, protective urges around anyone else, but with Lennox? I'm already obsessed.

I hand her my helmet and help her fasten it beneath her chin. She's so damn cute, I have to kiss her nose. She grins at me, and goddamn, my heart grows three sizes. I hop on my bike and instruct Lennox to swing her leg over and scoot up close to me.

It's too damn good having her riding behind me. She wraps her arms around my waist, pressing her curves against my back. My dick throbs back to life, but I manage to take a breath and calm down. I need to deliver my precious cargo home safely. Then I need to figure out how to make her mine forever.

Chapter 5

Lennox

My Saturday morning alarm goes off, but I've been awake for thirty minutes. I'm lying here in bed, smiling to myself as I replay everything that happened yesterday.

Ace kissed me. Everywhere.

My cheeks heat at the memory of his tongue gliding through my folds, flicking my most sensitive flesh and sucking until I surrendered to his touch. God, I hardly recognize myself. We broke all sorts of rules by mauling each other in the back hallway, but I made sure to clean and sanitize everything. Maybe I can get Ace to do it again sometime...

I sit up in bed, realizing for the first time that I don't have Ace's number. I don't know where he lives or how to contact him. Was that on purpose? Did Ace not want me to find him?

Old doubts and insecurities wrap around my lungs, squeezing until I can barely breathe.

No, I tell myself. Ace isn't like that. If all he wanted was to get off... well, he failed. He got me off, alright. A few times. But he never gave me the chance to repay the favor. Not that I would have any idea how to do that, but I'd try anything to give Ace the same pleasure he gave me.

Which means I need to see him again.

I settle back down in bed, snuggling into the soft blankets as I try to think of a plan. I have a rare day off from the coffee shop, and I'm going to take advantage of it.

Thinking back over what I know about Ace, the only helpful piece of information is that he gets his bike worked on at Dirty Gears. I'm sure I won't be lucky enough to drop by and bump into him, but maybe one of the mechanics knows how I can contact Ace.

The only problem is, I don't have a good excuse to go to a motorcycle garage. I don't have a bike, car, or any mode of transportation I could take to "get it looked at," so I'll need a different way in.

And then it dawns on me.

"Cookies!" I say out loud, throwing off the covers and leaping out of bed.

Who doesn't love cookies? If I show up with a batch of my double chocolate chunk cookies, maybe no one will ask questions. They'll be too distracted by the magical melt-in-your-mouth cookies. That's when I can ask about Ace. Plus, bringing cookies to hard-working mechanics can be my good deed for the day. It's perfect.

I hop in the shower, taking time to shave everywhere and wash my hair. Hey, a girl can never be too prepared, right? Especially when she has the attention of the sexiest man ever to walk the face of the earth.

After throwing on leggings and a t-shirt, I get to work on the cookies.

My chest tightens as my heart squeezes up painfully, and I concentrate on taking a full breath. My aunt loved baking. She taught me the basics when I was ten, and then we started working through all of her old family recipes. By fifteen, we were creating our own masterpieces.

Even though it hurts, I smile through the tears threatening to spill down my cheeks. I want to hang on to these precious memories of my aunt and not let my grief overshadow them. Baking is an activity we loved to do together, and I know she'd be happy to see me elbow-deep in cookie dough.

I go over the recipe in my head while getting out all the ingredients I need. I get lost in the mixing and measuring, and before I know it, the oven timer is going off for the last batch of cookies.

My mouth waters as I take them out of the oven, noting the perfectly gold-brown edges and still-soft doughy center. They'll bake a little more on the hot sheet pan, and in a few minutes, they'll be absolute chewy perfection.

Letting the cookies cool a bit, I go to my closet and pick out what I hope is a cute outfit. Fifteen minutes later, I'm heading out the door with a basket full of cookies. I chose a light-yellow dress with a daisy floral pattern and lace trim around the collar and hemline. The fabric tickles my knees as I walk down the sidewalk toward Dirty Gears.

By the time I reach the motorcycle shop, I've nearly talked myself out of the whole thing. What if Ace doesn't want to see me? What if he thinks I'm being clingy by trying to find him? Oh, God, what if he thinks I'm some crazy stalker like Charlie?

I pause, my feet stuck in place as I swallow back shame and embarrassment. Am I making a fool out of myself?

"Your presence is very much wanted."

Ace's words from the other day filter into my brain, banishing all other thoughts.

I breathe in his certainty, remembering how he held me, the taste of his kiss, and the way my body responded to his touch. If I want more of Ace, I'm going to have to be brave and ask for it. Something tells me he hasn't let anyone get close to him in a long time, if ever. I want to be the one he tells all his secrets to. I want to heal the wounds he carries around deep in his soul.

But first, I need to find him again.

Scraping up every bit of confidence I can find, I square my shoulders and march through the front door of Dirty Gears.

I'm hit with the scent of gasoline, rubber, and oil. Tools bang and clang in the background and the sound of metal on metal lets me know these men are hard at work.

The lobby is neat and tidy, with a front desk, chairs, a coffee maker, and a TV hung up in one corner.

"You lost?" someone asks from behind me. I spin around, looking up at a tall man covered in lean muscle.

"Um..."

The man crosses his arms, and I notice the noise coming from the garage has stopped. I peer around the man currently glaring at me and see several men staring at me through the large window overlooking the garage.

"You got a bike that needs fixing?" he asks, prompting me to say something.

This was a bad idea. What was I thinking? That I'd waltz in here and shout *cookies* and have everyone eating out of my hand?

My brain decides that's exactly what we're going to do.

"Cookies!" I blurt, holding up the basket and pulling back the kitchen towel I used to cover it.

I didn't realize the men from the garage were heading our way until the door swings open, banging against the wall. I jump, then let out a startled laugh when four huge tatted-up bikers jog over and shove their hands into the basket, pulling out at least three cookies each.

"Animals," the man standing in front of me says with a scoff. He rolls his eyes, then looks at me more suspiciously this time. "Why are you giving us cookies? Are they laced with something?"

"What? God, no," I'm quick to answer. I notice none of the guys stop chowing down on their cookies, even with the mention of poison. "I was hoping I'd see Ace here. Do any of you know him?"

One of the guys stops mid-bite and gives me a once-over. "Lennox?" he asks with a full mouth.

"Yeah," I respond with a nod, unsure why this man knows my name.

"Well, shit," he says with a chuckle. "Ace got himself a proper lady. I knew that dopey smile on his face was about a woman. I'm Reaper, by the way. President of this here club."

He talked about me to his friends? That has to be a good sign.

"Good to meet you," I hedge, holding out the basket for him to take another cookie. "About Ace... I don't even have his number. I thought maybe one of you could–"

"Lennox?" Ace shouts from somewhere in the garage.

Oh, crap. He sounds angry. Maybe this was a horrible idea after all. Cookies? A floral dress? Nothing screams innocent little kid like sweets and daisies.

Ace appears in the doorway, his shoulders so wide they take up nearly the entire opening. He storms toward me, the look in his intense eyes impossible to read. Is he angry? Embarrassed of me?

Oh, God, please let the floor open up and swallow me whole.

His massive frame moves with surprising grace, closing the distance between us in three long strides. My mouth gapes as he wraps his fingers around the basket full of cookies, yanks it out of my grip, and shoves it in Reaper's hands.

I don't have time to wonder what the heck he's doing before he circles his arms around me and hauls me into his chest, covering my lips with his in a devastating kiss.

I forget everything else except this kiss. Ace parts my lips with his, sliding his tongue inside my mouth and licking me in slow, teasing strokes. I melt against him, hardly realizing we're moving until Ace cups my ass and guides me to wrap my legs around him.

Somewhere in the background, I hear faint whistles and shouts from the other bikers, but I don't care. Ace is here, and he's kissing me, and everything is right in my world once more.

"Where are we going?" I ask as Ace continues to carry me across the parking lot.

"Somewhere more private," he says with a low growl. I can feel the vibrations in my core, making my thighs shake as I cling to his massive frame. "Fuck me, Lennox. You feel too good."

Ace barely finishes that thought before his mouth is on mine, kissing me with such intensity I can barely breathe. I don't mind. Who needs air when you have a sexy, possessive biker making you melt with every swipe of his tongue?

He eventually breaks the kiss, setting me down in front of his bike. Ace looks down at my dress and frowns. I instinctively wrap my arms around my waist and take a step back. I thought my outfit was cute, but now I realize it's childish.

Ace reaches out, wrapping his fingers around my wrist and tugging me toward him. "What are you thinking about right now?" he asks as he pulls me into his warm, comforting chest.

I bury my head in his shirt, breathing in his calming, familiar scent. Ace runs a hand up and down my spine, each stroke relaxing me even more.

Geeze, I'm a mess. Ace has me on edge, but not in a bad way. It's all overwhelming, and I'm afraid I'm way more invested in us than Ace is. I don't want to look like a silly girl with a crush.

"Lennox?" Ace murmurs, trying to peel me off his chest. I burrow down further into his embrace, making him chuckle.

"The dress is stupid," I mumble.

"What?" This time, Ace manages to tip my head back so we're face to face.

I shrug, trying to play it cool. We're way past saving face, but a girl has to try. "You're probably used to women who wear leather mini skirts and lingerie, and here I am in this dumpy dress–"

"I love your dress," Ace interrupts. The sincerity in his voice nearly brings tears to my eyes. "It's perfect because it's on *you*. That's why I feel bad about getting it dirty."

"Huh?" I take a step back and look down at my dress. Sure enough, there's a grease stain on the skirt and a black smear of something over my left breast.

I grin at Ace, who looks genuinely upset about ruining my dress. "I think I like being dirty with you," I murmur in what I hope is a seductive voice. I have no idea where this wanton woman came from, but I like her.

Ace groans and steps closer to me, crowding me up against his bike. I rest against it as the huge, muscular man with tattoos up and down his arms leans over me. His frame blocks out the sun, and the only thing I can see are those deep blue eyes.

He rests his forehead on mine in a surprisingly sweet gesture. Ace takes a shaky breath, then wraps his arms around me and pulls me in for a hug. I thought he was going to kiss the air from my lungs, but this is nice, too.

I snuggle into his chest once more, soaking up every drop of attention this man is willing to give me. I swear I can feel his insecurity as he clings to me, almost like he's afraid I'll run away if he lets go.

Squeezing my arms around Ace's back, I silently tell him I'm not going anywhere. As long as he wants me near, I'll be right by his side.

"Can I show you my favorite place?" Ace whispers onto the top of my head before placing the sweetest kiss there.

"Yes, please!" I respond, pressing my lips to his chest, right over his heart. Ace looks down at me with a mix of confusion and awe. It breaks my heart. Has no one ever been nice to this man? That changes right now.

Ace puts his helmet on me and fastens the strap beneath my chin. He gives me that lopsided smile I love so much, and I return it, hoping to see more of his happiness soon. He hops on his bike with practiced ease, then instructs me again on how to throw my leg over and scoot up.

I've been on Ace's bike before, but I'm still not used to the power of his vehicle when it starts up. The bike roars to life, the entire thing vibrating and humming and making my heart race.

"Hang on tight, baby," Ace shouts over his shoulder.

I wrap my arms around him, feeling the muscles of his torso flex as he revs the engine. I wiggle in my seat, scooting up close enough to press my thighs, my chest, my everything right up against Ace's back.

A soft moan escapes my lips when Ace takes off. *Holy crap*, the thunder of the bike settles between my thighs, making my clit pulse. It's good... *so good...*

I rock back and forth, hardly aware that I'm grinding down on the bike seat. I angle my hips, digging my fingers into Ace's abs and suppressing another moan when I rub my swollen, sensitive clit against the seat.

"Fuck," I hear Ace growl. "You like that?"

I press my forehead against his back and nod my head, tightening my thighs around the outsides of his legs.

Ace picks up speed, zipping through the sparse traffic in town. I'm so freaking turned on, so raw and on edge, I think I might come without him even touching me.

We pull into an empty gravel lot, and Ace instructs me to get off the bike. I pout but do as he says, my legs a little wobbly from the ride and my crippling lust. Ace scoots back in the seat, then drags me closer, lifting me into his lap so I'm straddling him.

"So damn sexy," he grunts before covering my lips with his.

The bike is still running, the vibrations coursing through my body and winding me up more and more with each passing second. Ace cups my ass, pulling me closer and grinding me against the solid length in his jeans.

Whoa. I made him that hard? He must be massive *everywhere.*

I tear myself away from his kiss, tipping my head back to let out a whimpered cry. Ace licks and nips at my exposed neck, driving me wild. The sensation of his teeth and tongue on my flesh is overwhelming, combined with the vibrations of the bike beneath me and his huge, hard cock rubbing me just right...

I come with a gasp, holding my breath as a wave of pleasure breaks over my body, trickling into my veins, and weaving itself in and out of my cells. Every muscle tenses, all of my energy pushing, pulling, pulsing through me as I fall apart in Ace's arms.

Collapsing on his chest, I bury my face into the side of his neck, melting into his embrace. He wraps his arms around me, holding me close while I tremble out the last of my orgasm.

"Holy shit," he breathes, making me laugh.

"I think that's my line," I tease, though I'm still out of breath.

Ace kisses my nose and forehead, then helps me off the bike. I'm still a bit wobbly on my feet, but Ace slides an arm around my waist and tucks me into his side, leading us up a little embankment.

When we get to the top, I'm shocked to see our little town of Haven laid out before us. The trees proudly display their fall colors, making the landscape a kaleidoscope of orange, red, yellow, and brown. It's stunning.

"Wow," I whisper as I gaze out over the scene. I can pick out a few businesses, including The Grind.

"Yeah," Ace agrees, stepping up behind me and looping his arms around my waist. I lean back against him, sighing with contentment. He rests his chin on top of my head, and I smile, knowing we fit together perfectly. "I come up here when I need a different perspective."

I nod but don't say anything. I'm beyond honored that Ace shared this with me. He might not be the most talkative person, but he's showing me more and more of his heart, whether he knows it or not.

"Sometimes..." he starts, then pauses, taking a deep breath. I stay perfectly still, not wanting to scare him away from saying what he needs to say. "Sometimes, I have bad dreams. Nightmares or whatever the fuck," he says softly. I can hear the shame in his voice, and it only makes me love him more.

Love? There's no time to unpack that right now. Not when Ace is breaking himself open for me.

"I usually spend at least one night a week out here, sleeping under the stars. It's the best view of town and the night sky. It's cheesy, I guess, but my problems don't feel as big when I'm looking up at the universe, you know?"

"It's not cheesy," I insist, spinning around in his arms. "It's beautiful. I'm sorry you have nightmares. I used to have them after my aunt passed away last year."

Ace's dark blue eyes turn soft as he presses a kiss to my forehead. "I'm so sorry, angel. I had no idea."

"I'm working through it," I tell him with a smile. "It still hurts, but I'm trying not to let grief steal my beautiful memories of her. That's part of why I do the acts of kindness thing. It gives me perspective, too, in a way. I can focus on other people and make their day a little brighter. It makes my day brighter, too."

I hoped my words would put Ace at ease, but he looks away from me, something close to shame in his eyes.

"You're too damn good for me," he grunts.

"What? No, that's not true." Ace still won't look at me, so I gather up all my courage and cup his face in my hands. His eyes latch onto mine, and the torment I see swirling in their depths brings tears to my eyes. "Let me show you how much I want you," I murmur before kissing my man.

He groans into my kiss, making me feel powerful and sexy. I pull my lips away from his and trail kisses down his throat. I get a wicked idea, one that surprises me and turns me on at the same time.

Before I can second guess myself, I kneel on the grass in front of Ace, giving him what I hope is a sexy smile. I have no idea what I'm doing, I just know I want to do it. I *need* to do it. Ace looks down at me with wide eyes, dark with lust.

"You don't have to—" His words die on his lips, swallowed up by a loud groan when I rub my palm up and down his huge, hard dick.

I look up at him, satisfied beyond reason that his face is twisted up in pleasure. Working quickly, I undo his belt and zipper, eager to touch him the way he touched me.

"Wow," I whisper, feeling foolish as soon as the word leaves my mouth. I'm sure I look and sound stupid, but I can't help it. He's huge. I can barely wrap my fingers around his thickness. A desperate, devilish ache rises in my core when I see a drop of white, pearly liquid form on the tip of his throbbing cock.

I lean forward and lick it up, gasping at the salty, earthy flavor. Ace growls, which makes me moan and wrap my lips around him. God, he barely fits in my mouth, but I want more. I swirl my tongue around the head, rubbing my tongue along the little slit on top. He grunts, sounding almost like he's in pain.

I keep exploring him, licking the large vein on the underside of his cock, teasing him with kisses, then finally swallowing him down again, choking on his length. Ace tangles his fingers in my hair, holding me still. I can't tell if he wants me to stop or go deeper. I know what I want, and I don't want to stop.

"Lennox," he growls, tightening his hold on my hair. The strands pull against my scalp, the slight sting hitting me right between my legs. "Fuck, you're incredible."

I beam up at him, unreasonably proud of his praise. It makes me want more. More of his words, more of his cock, just... more. Relaxing my jaw, I slide down another inch, then another, until he hits the back of my throat.

Ace cups the side of my face, holding me still. I look up at him and see a need so great, so desperate, I know I'm going to do whatever he asks of me to satisfy him. Slowly, Ace moves his hips, pulling out of me and then pressing back in. I suck him down, hollowing out my cheeks as he takes control, fucking my mouth.

"Jesus," he grunts, snapping his hips. He's thrusting in and out of me faster now, rougher than before. I take all of it, everything he's giving me. I feel a surge of pride when he starts shaking, clearly losing control.

My hands move on their own, reaching up to grab his ass and keep him deep inside my mouth. Ace lets out a string of curse words as his dick twitches and swells up. I suck him down further, the tip of his cock popping into the back of my throat. Ace trembles almost violently, then bursts inside me, his hot cum trickling down my throat in forceful waves. I moan and drink down every last drop before licking him clean.

Sitting back on my heels, I wipe my mouth with the back of my hand and look up at this beast of a man. He's breathing heavily and staring at me like I'm a goddess. I feel like one at this moment. His goddess.

Ace helps me up and thrusts his tongue inside my mouth, kissing the breath from my lungs. "So beautiful," he murmurs, wrapping his arms around me.

I kiss the center of his chest, then beam up at him, glowing from his praise and the fact that I could give him so much pleasure.

After a few minutes, we both catch our breath. Ace gets himself back together, giving me a devilish smirk as he tucks his half-hard dick back into his pants.

"So... have I earned your phone number yet?" I tease. Ace frowns, then looks stricken. "I mean, if not–"

"Of course," he interjects. "I just feel bad that you didn't have it before. Dammit, I'm doing this all wrong," he mutters as he wipes a hand down his face.

"Hey," I say in a gentle voice. "It's okay. There are no rules, just us."

Ace looks up at me, giving me a small little smile. I'll take it.

"Still, I think I owe you a date by now, don't you think?"

"A date?"

"Yeah. It can be low-key. Dinner at my place?"

"Really?"

Ace smiles, a real, full smile, and God, he's breathtaking. He stalks toward me, wrapping his fingers around my hips and pulling me flush against his solid frame. "Really," he whispers, rubbing his nose against mine in the softest touch.

"I can't wait," I tell him truthfully.

Ace loads me up on the back of his bike and winds his way through town until we get to my apartment. I don't want to leave him, but I feel better now that I have his number.

Now I just need to figure out how to seduce him for real and make him fall for me, too.

Chapter 6

Ace

I pull at the tie knotted around my neck, loosening it enough so I can take a full breath. Looking at myself in the mirror, I try turning my grimace into a smile. It doesn't feel right. None of this feels right.

When Lennox joked about earning my phone number, I wanted to punch myself in the goddamn nose. She must think I'm a savage. I've tasted her pussy and let her suck me off but never thought to give her my number? *Moron.*

To make up for my brutish ways, I wanted to pull out all the stops tonight, including a crisp, white, brand-new button-down shirt and a tie. The older woman at the men's clothing store had mercy on me when I showed up earlier this afternoon. She helped me pick out a tie that supposedly matches my eyes.

But now, I feel like a fraud. I've never done this shit. Never been on a proper date. Never wined and dined anyone. Never wanted to impress another living soul, but now, I have the unquenchable need to be everything for Lennox. She deserves the whole goddamn world at her feet. I want to prove to her that I'm more than an oaf on a bike who can pack a punch.

But this shirt is scratchy, this damn tie is strangling me, and the shoes I bought earlier to match my new dress slacks are giving me blisters. They didn't have anything in my size, so I took the closest thing. Big mistake. How do people wear these things?

I'm about to tear everything off and walk around naked, but the timer on the oven goes off. I hardly ever cook. Most of my meals come from the diner, the clubhouse, or a can. Fortunately, Reaper's girl, Arabelle, gave me a simple recipe for chicken and rice. It's nothing fancy, but at least I won't burn the house down.

Stomping out to the kitchen, I pause and take a deep breath, pushing back my dark thoughts and insecurities. They're always present, but I don't want to drag Lennox through all my bullshit. She doesn't deserve that. Besides, she'll figure out soon enough that I'm trash. I've always been trash.

I've moved halfway across the damn country, but I'll always be the dirty kid scraping by on the streets of LA. The shit I had to do to earn money, to have a warm meal... it's too gruesome to think about, let alone talk about.

The timer goes off again, jerking me out of my thoughts. It's too late to cancel on her now. My chest tightens when I think about sending my angel away. If I hurt her in any way, or Christ, made her cry, I couldn't live with myself.

I'll always be here for Lennox. It's my duty to protect her, to make sure she's safe and happy. When she inevitably leaves me for someone worthy of her love, I'll still be here. I'll be a miserable fuck, but I'll be at her beck and call until the day I die. There's no use fighting it.

I pull the casserole dish out of the oven and peel back the tin foil, pleasantly surprised at how good it looks and smells. Placing it on top of the stove to cool, I gather plates and silverware to set the table.

My doorbell rings, and I jump, dropping the fork and spoon I had in my hand. I curse as they clatter onto the floor. *Off to a great start.*

Stumbling my way to the door, I wipe my sweaty hands on my pants, then remember I'm wearing my nice, new dress slacks. Probably shouldn't be getting my bodily fluids all over them.

Before I lose my courage completely, I open the door. *Fuck.* Lennox is more gorgeous than I remember. Her silky auburn hair hangs around her shoulders in soft waves, and her bright, golden eyes shine at me. She's wearing a lacy light blue dress that hits just above her knees. The material hugs her breasts, showing off a hint of cleavage. Jesus, I want to stare at her all day and rip the fabric from her body so I can worship her curves with my fingers and tongue.

"Excuse me, sir, is Ace here?" Lennox says with a sassy grin.

I give her my best smirk, but my heart is thundering in my chest. Does she think I look stupid? What was I thinking, trying to pass off as a proper gentleman?

"Ace?" Lennox says again, softer this time.

"Yeah, yeah," I answer, my breath choppy and my words forced. "You... are breathtaking," I mumble, immediately feeling foolish. She's so much more than breathtaking, but I can't seem to get anything right tonight.

"You clean up pretty good yourself," Lennox says easily.

Some of the tension drains from my muscles, but I'm still on edge. "Do you like it?" *Dammit, why did I say that?* It's true, I'm desperate for her approval, but I don't want to be pathetic about it.

Lennox beams up at me, taking a step closer. I step back, and she follows, smiling at me the whole time. Once we're inside my house, Lennox wraps her fingers around my tie and pulls me down for a kiss.

Her taste explodes on my tongue, banishing all other thoughts. I draw her closer, tangling my fingers in her hair and angling her head so I can kiss her deeper. I need more, need her scent in my lungs, her soothing touch, and whispered words.

When we break for air, Lennox tugs at my tie again, leading me into the living room like a puppy on a leash. Fuck, for this woman, I am. A lovesick puppy.

"Where are we going?" I ask with a chuckle.

"Here," she says, stopping in front of the couch.

She pushes on my chest, motioning for me to sit. I gladly obey. Lennox surprises me by climbing on my lap and straddling me. My hands automatically find her hips, and I rock her on top of me, teasing both of us. Lennox walks her fingers up my tie, then tugs at the knot, loosening the torture device and tossing it behind her.

"That feels better," I groan, taking a deep breath.

My woman smiles, then goes for the buttons on my shirt. I raise an eyebrow, but I'm sure as hell not going to stop her.

"I like you in whatever you wear," she says as she pops open another button. "But you look uncomfortable."

"Not quite used to the tie yet," I grunt.

"Ace," Lennox whispers, pausing her unbuttoning to cup the side of my face.

God, this woman's sweet touch will be my undoing. No one has ever treated me with such gentleness. I don't deserve it.

"Hey," she says with a firmer voice. "I want *you*. As you are. No frills, no dressy clothes, just you."

"I'm not a good man," I blurt, breaking eye contact with her.

"I don't believe that," she murmurs, guiding my face to meet hers again. She leans forward, brushing her lips against mine in the sweetest kiss.

"I've lived a rough life, Lennox," I whisper.

"You did what you had to do to survive. And now you're here, with me. Isn't that enough?" Lennox presses another kiss to my lips, the tip of her tongue snaking out and teasing me before she pulls back.

"Of course, you're enough. It's just... fuck, I've... I've done some shit. Bad shit." I turn my head away from her, but my girl places her hands on either side of my face, drawing my attention back.

"You've also been kind to me and protected me when I needed it. You've been sweet, even when you're growling."

I grunt, making her giggle. Jesus, I want to bottle that sound so I can replay it over and over once she leaves me for good.

"I'm serious," she continues. "Whatever you've been through, whatever life made you do, it all led you to this moment. So, what are you going to do with it?"

Those ethereal eyes hit me with such intensity and sincerity that I have no choice but to believe her. The angel sits on my lap, her lips slightly parted as she waits for my response.

I lean forward, resting my forehead on hers. Closing my eyes, I breathe in her sugary sweet smell, letting it ground me. "Will you let me show you how good I'll be to you?"

"Only if you let me show you how good I'll be to you, too." Lennox smiles, then nibbles on her bottom lip.

I can't hold back any longer. This woman is mine, and for whatever reason, she wants me. I capture her lips in a drugging kiss, thrusting my tongue inside her mouth and claiming her with every stroke. She moans as she rolls her hips, hitting my thick cock just right. I stand with my girl in my arms, loving the weight of her and how she fits in my embrace.

"What about dinner?" Lennox pants once she breaks for air.

"It'll taste better warmed up," I lie through my teeth.

Lennox giggles, but I cut her off with another kiss, swallowing the sound and making it my own.

I set my precious girl down in front of my bed, though my lips and hands never leave her body. I smooth my fingers over the curve of her hips, the dip of her waist, and finally, cup her juicy breasts. She tips her head back, gasping when I squeeze her sensitive flesh.

"Goddamn," I growl, nipping at her neck, her collarbone, her exposed cleavage.

"More, Ace," she whimpers, her hands fisting my shirt and trying to pull it off.

I take a step back, chuckling when Lennox sways on her feet. I undo the last few buttons of my shirt and let it slip off my shoulders. My woman stares at me, her pupils blown wide as she studies my chest. I have more than a few scars, though most are covered with tattoos.

"You're so... hot." Lennox's cheeks turn pink, but she can't seem to look away from me. I don't mind.

"Thanks, angel," I say with a smirk. "Now it's your turn."

Lennox lifts her arms, and I grin at her eagerness. I love that she's no longer shy around me. It killed me the other day when she thought

I didn't like her dress. Shit, I guess I was the same way with my attempt at fancy clothes. Maybe we're not as different as I first thought.

I skim my hands up her legs, shoving up her dress as my fingers reach higher, higher, higher...

"Oh, god," Lennox moans as soon as I rub my hand over her damp panties.

"So fucking wet for me," I growl, my dick throbbing behind my zipper.

"Mmhm," she says with a nod.

"So damn eager."

"Yup," my girl confirms, making me laugh. I don't think I've smiled this much in my entire life.

I drag her dress up and over her head, followed quickly by her bra and matching panties. When she's completely naked before me, I brush my knuckles over her bare breasts, teasing her nipples and driving her crazy.

"So beautiful," I whisper, kissing the corner of her lips. "So fucking *mine*," I grunt, kissing her with all the passion and intensity I have for her.

Lennox digs her fingernails into my shoulders as she clings to me, and I groan at the slight sting. Pulling back slightly, I guide her to lay down on my bed. She does but then sits up on her knees when I start unbuckling my belt. I don't think she's aware of it, but she's staring right at my dick, licking her pouty lips. *Jesus.*

I rid myself of the last of my clothes, making a note to burn them as soon as I get a chance.

Lennox whimpers and reaches for me, placing her palms on my bare chest. I close my eyes and tilt my head back, pumping my swollen dick while she takes her time exploring me, exploring what belongs to her.

Lennox drags one hand down my abs, lower, fuck, lower, until she's gripping my cock, taking over for me.

"Jesus," I grit out, snapping my eyes open and looking down at her little hand that can barely fit around me. "Angel, I'm gonna need you to stop if you want this to last longer than ten seconds."

Lennox gasps in surprise, biting her bottom lip and giving me a devious smile. Then the little minx bends down and sucks my cock into her mouth, swirling her tongue around the tip and licking up the steady stream of precum pouring out of me.

I can't stop my hips from bucking and my hands gripping the sides of her head, holding her steady while I ease my way in and out of her mouth.

"Gotta stop, baby. Gotta pull back," I growl, though I can't seem to let her go.

I finally pry my hands away from her, groaning when she releases my dick from her mouth with a pop. I push her back onto the mattress and climb on top of her, immediately seeking out her lips and spearing my tongue inside her mouth. I don't give a fuck that I taste myself on her. It makes me feel like a fucking king that this goddess sucked my cock and now wants me inside her.

"Please," she whispers, spreading her legs wider for me and tilting her hips so my hard, heavy length settles between her warm, wet folds.

I thrust along her slit, gathering her juices and letting them coat my cock. Leaning down, I brush my nose along her neck and then kiss her lips softly. "This is your first time, right, beautiful?"

"Yeah," she whispers, searing me with her intense golden eyes. I look for any hints of doubt or fear, but I only see lust. Lust and a longing that matches my own. She wants to be filled as much as I want to fill her, and not just physically. She wants more. And I want to give her everything.

I kiss her pulse point, which is pounding rapidly against my lips. Lifting my head, I look at my beautiful, sweet, too fucking pure woman, soaking up everything about her at this moment. Resting my forehead on hers, I line myself up with her entrance, pushing the tip inside.

Lennox squeezes her eyes shut, and I kiss her closed eyelids. "Look at me, sweet girl. Look at me while I claim you."

Her eyes pop open, and I slide another inch inside her tight, sopping wet channel. Lennox whimpers and digs her fingernails into my shoulders. I stop, not wanting to hurt her, but Lennox surprises the fuck out of me by bucking her hips and shoving her pussy further down my cock.

"Yessss..." she moans.

"Fuck. Look at you, so eager for my dick. This what you need?" I pull back and push inside her again, going a little deeper this time until I reach her barrier.

She tenses in my arms but then nods her head, wiggling her hips and making me lose my goddamn mind. "You. You are what I need."

That's it. I snap my hips forward, tearing through her innocence and claiming this cunt as my new home.

"Mine," I growl as I bury myself deep inside her.

Lennox whimpers and locks her ankles behind my back, holding me close. "Yes, I need it, I need it," she whispers over and over.

I stay still, letting us both feel this connection for the first time. My cock twitches and leaks more precum, but I grit my teeth and hold back my orgasm, waiting until she loosens up and gets used to my size.

Her walls pulse around me, and I pull back, staring down between us and savoring her creamy white cum mixed with my own and the evidence of her virginity. Christ, I almost fall right off the edge at the sight.

I fill her up again, slowly working my cock in and out of her pussy. Lennox grips the back of my neck and pulls me down for a frantic kiss while circling her hips and meeting me thrust for thrust. I hook my hand under her right knee and pull her leg up and to the side, opening her up even more and switching up the angle. Thrusting back inside in long, rough strokes, I scrape my cock along her walls in search of her secret little treasure.

"Ohmy*god*!" Lennox cries out.

"There it is," I grunt, hammering into that spot while she convulses beneath me.

"Ace! I can't. I can't, I..."

She shakes and tenses and gasps for air, but I don't let up. I keep striking that same spot, over and over, so hard I push her up the mattress with each vicious stroke. Some part of me knows I should slow down, be gentle with her since it's her first time, but fuck, looking at her face twisted up in pleasure makes me drive into her harder, faster, giving her more, needing more for myself.

"Come for me, Lennox. Let go," I groan, dipping my head to suck on her bouncing tits.

"I want to. I want to, I-I w-want..."

"Do it," I growl, rearing back and throwing her legs over my shoulders.

I pound that little pussy over and over, groaning with her as she squeezes me so goddamn tight. Lennox claws at my chest and screams out her orgasm. She's ruined, coming apart beneath me, squirming and tensing and trying to get away from this intense pleasure. I hold her in place, making her feel all of it, every single second.

Before she has a chance to recover, I pull out of her and grip her hips, flipping her around and positioning her on her hands and knees.

"Fuck," I groan, sliding my hands up and down her back and squeezing the soft flesh of her ass. I pull her cheeks apart and slam my thick dick into her pulsing little pussy, growling at the sloppy wet sounds we're making as I fuck my woman hard and fast.

She moans and arches her back, wedging my cock deeper inside her. "I'm so close already. I'm so close..."

I lean over her, covering her entire body with my large frame. I rest my hands on top of hers, caging her in and lacing our fingers together while I grind my cock into her swollen, beat-up little pussy.

"Harder, please, so hard...so good, please."

Her desperate cries have my balls drawing up tight as fire races through my veins. "Whatever you want, angel. I'll give you everything."

I rut into her, tearing her cunt apart. Lennox throws her head back, resting it on my shoulder. I turn my head and suck on her neck, holding still inside of her as she comes. It's quiet and brutal, the way her release overwhelms her.

Feeling her orgasm pulse around my dick is incredible. I fuck her through it, so damn hard, as she sobs beneath me and soaks my cock. The bed creaks, and the headboard slams against the wall, but I can't stop.

Lennox cries out her pleasure as she comes again, taking me with her. My orgasm overwhelms me, squeezing the air from my lungs and making my ears ring. Eventually, I collapse on top of Lennox, holding myself deep inside her snug little pussy while she milks the last of my cum.

We lie there, a sweaty, tangled mess until I roll to the side. I drape Lennox's limp body over my chest and wrap my arms around her, tucking her head under my chin.

"You okay?" I whisper, kissing the top of her head.

"Holy hell," she breathes, making me laugh. "Do that again," she says.

"Do what again? Fuck you? Give me a few minutes." I chuckle.

"No, I mean... laugh. I like your laugh." I freeze at her words and swallow down the lump in my throat. "But yeah, you can fuck me again, too," she sighs, snuggling deeper into my chest.

I stroke her back and play with her wild, messy hair. I love knowing I caused her auburn curls to tangle and stick to the back of her sweaty neck. I love knowing I'm the one who made her sweat, made her come, over and over. Fucking hell, I'm almost ready to go again.

Looking down at my woman, I see her eyes are closed, and her breaths are deep and even. Pride wells up in my chest, knowing I gave her so much pleasure and wore her out. I love that she feels safe enough to fall asleep with me.

I need to figure out how to keep her here for good.

Chapter 7

Lennox

I slowly blink awake, realizing how bright it is outside. I never sleep in this late. Rolling over, I look at the clock, only to remember I'm not in my bed. I'm not in my apartment at all.

A smile parts my lips as I reminisce about how it felt to have Ace move deep inside me, how his midnight blue eyes locked onto mine and never let go as he watched me fall apart for him over and over.

Sighing contentedly, I wake up a little more. I'm in a huge bed surrounded by soft sheets and Ace's crisp, comforting scent. I look over, expecting the man who took my virginity to be right next to me. Panic floods through me when I see I'm alone.

I throw the covers off and bolt out of bed, my breaths growing choppy as I paw around the room for my clothes.

Oh, my god, did he leave me already? Was I that terrible last night? I thought we shared something incredible but was I being naive?

Before my thoughts spiral completely, I hear pots and pans clanging in what I assume is the kitchen. I didn't get much of a tour before falling into bed with my big, sexy biker, but I don't have any regrets. I hope he doesn't, either. Only one way to find out.

I find one of Ace's t-shirts folded up on his dresser, so I throw it on, loving how big it is on me. I could put a belt around the middle and wear it as a dress if I wanted to. I'm obsessed enough to sincerely consider it.

Opening the bedroom door, I peer out into the hallway, noting that the entire floor is made of gorgeous, glossy oak. Not what I was expecting, but I like it. I spot the bathroom across the hall and dip inside to freshen up a bit before continuing my journey.

Following the noise, I find the kitchen a few moments later. I lean against the door frame, taking in the sight of my man cooking breakfast in nothing but a pair of gray sweatpants. *Yes, please.*

As if sensing my presence, Ace looks over his shoulder, grinning when he sees me. Good lord, his smile... it gives me all kinds of crazy ideas like staying here with him forever and asking him to be the father of my children.

Reel it in, I remind myself. Ace may be rough and closed off to the world, but I know it's because he's trying to protect himself. I'm not sure who or what broke his heart, only that I want to be the one to collect all the pieces and stitch them back together.

"Come here, angel," he commands, his grin turning into a devilish smirk.

Blue eyes darken with lust as they roam up and down my body. I've never considered myself sexy or seductive, but the way Ace looks at me makes me feel like a damn porn star. I sashay over to him, swinging my hips as I go. Ace lets out a low rumble as he prowls toward me, his large hands wrapping around my curves as he hauls me into his chest and takes my mouth in a demanding kiss.

I loop my arms around his neck and kiss him back with all the passion and urgency he's giving me. Ace smooths his hands up and down my sides, squeezing and caressing every inch of me like he can't get enough.

Breaking the kiss, I tilt my head back and gulp down air. Ace nuzzles into the side of my neck, then surprises me by spinning me around so my back is flush with his front. Slowly, he slides his hands under the hem of my shirt, exploring and teasing me with every tender touch. The tips of his fingers tickle my thighs, my stomach, and finally, my breasts.

"That's it, beautiful," he rasps, his lips brushing the shell of my ear. "Love feeling these tits. Love your curvy little body. So damn tempting walking around in my clothes like this."

I nod, falling under the spell of his magical touch and filthy words. Resting my hands on the counter in front of me, I arch my back, rubbing my ass against his massive erection. Ace growls as he pinches my nipples, sending a tremor down my spine.

A moan escapes my lips as Ace continues exploring me with his hands. He slowly drags the oversized shirt up and off my body, the fabric tickling my skin and making me shiver.

Ace growls and bends me over the kitchen counter, palming my cheeks and spreading me wide open for him. He takes himself out and rubs his dick between my folds while I push back, trying to get him inside me again. I'm addicted to this man. I know he's the only one who will ever be able to satisfy my cravings.

I feel his lips on my lower back, slowly moving their way up my spine.

"Tell me what you want, beautiful," he whispers into my skin.

"You," I breathe.

"You have me, angel. Now, what do you want me to do to your gorgeous body?"

He continues to saw in and out of my folds, not penetrating me yet. I moan loudly, my pussy squeezing on nothing as it gushes over his cock.

"I want you to... fuck me, Ace."

He growls. "Tell me again." He snaps his hips, bumping my clit.

"*Fuck me,* Ace. I want to feel you tear me apart."

"Jesus, baby, love when you talk dirty," he grunts.

Ace pulls back and slams home, again and again, hitting me so deep I cry out with each thrust.

"You like that? Like my thick cock stretching out your perfect little pussy?"

"Mmhm..." I moan, pressing back into him, meeting him thrust for thrust. I squeeze my pussy each time he pulls out, loving how he groans and his breath hitches in his throat.

"Fuck, Lennox. Love being inside you. I'll never get enough. You're mine, angel. *Mine,*" he grunts as he picks up speed. He pushes me closer and closer to the edge, and just when I'm about to fall off into blinding pleasure, he pulls out.

"No!" I yell out in frustration.

The beastly biker laughs darkly and leans his huge, hard body over mine. "I'm not done with you yet, beautiful," he growls.

His words sink into my bloodstream, making me tremble in anticipation.

Ace walks us backward to one of the kitchen chairs and sits down, guiding me onto his lap so my back is facing his front and my legs are spread out on either side of his. Slowly, he lowers me down on top of his hard shaft.

"Oh, Ace, this is..." I have no words. Riding him backward feels so, *so* incredible. As I bounce up and down his long, hard length, I find I like being in control of our pleasure. I reach my hands behind me and tangle them in his hair, urging his head forward so he can kiss my neck.

"Fuck, that's it, beautiful. Ride my big dick. Fucking hell, you feel so good."

I lift and impale myself on him again and again. Ace's large hands cup my breasts as he kneads the soft flesh and pinches my nipples. One hand slowly slides down my ribs and torso, resting on the mound of soft curls above my pussy. Ace parts my folds and circles my clit, again and again, bringing me right back to the edge of my orgasm.

"Ace, right there, oh *god*, I can't hold on..."

I grind down on him, loving how his cock fills me, stretching and hitting every sensitive spot deep inside me.

"Let go. I've got you," he whispers before biting down on my shoulder.

I throw my head back and grip his hair as my body locks up and tenses, every muscle, every nerve pushed to the extreme, waiting for my permission to let go.

Ace pinches my clit, and I scream out my release, my body curling up and pitching forward with the force of my orgasm. Ace holds me steady with one hand on my breast, the other cupping my pussy as he fucks into me from below.

"Fuck, *fuck*, Lennox. Jesus, I'm coming with you, baby."

One orgasm rolls into another, and another until I'm a big ball of nerves, electrocuted with each thrust of Ace's hips.

I blink my eyes open as Ace places sweet kisses on my shoulder.

"Hey," he whispers. "You passed out there for a second." He smiles against my skin. "You okay?"

I giggle a little. He literally fucked me till I passed out. "Yeah, I'm good. I'm really good."

"Mmm, yes, you are," he mumbles, kissing my neck. His arms wrap around me and hold me close. "You're perfect. Let's get you dressed, and then I'll finish up breakfast."

I nod, though I don't move a muscle. I lean against Ace's bare chest, the sweat cooling on my body and making me shiver. He chuckles, kissing the side of my neck and standing with me in his arms. I giggle as he lifts me and carries me to his room.

Ten hours later, I still can't wipe the smile off my face. I've been at The Grind since one this afternoon, and it's almost closing time. I don't usually like the Saturday closing shift, but nothing can bring me down today. Not when my muscles still ache deliciously from my morning workout in the kitchen with Ace.

"Are you thinking dirty thoughts about your man again?" Maribel shouts from out in the lobby, broom in hand. I look up from where I'm wiping out the bakery case and see her accusatory glare. She smiles a second later, and I can't help but laugh.

"How did you know?" I ask in a hushed voice, even though no one else is here.

"Your cheeks are flushed, and you have a far-off, dreamy look in your gorgeous eyes. Plus, you're practically drooling," she jokes.

"I can't help it!"

"Uh-huh," she replies, a grin spreading across her face. "For real, I'm excited for you, Lennox. You deserve all the happiness in the world."

I smile at my friend and thank her before finishing my task.

Maribel turns off the open sign while I gather the last of the garbage from behind the counter. "I'm taking the trash out, and then we should be about finished!" I call out as I haul two garbage bags out the back door. Opening it with a swing of my hip, I step out into the ally, dragging the giant bags of trash with me.

The sun has almost set, the sky glowing bright orange like the embers of a dying fire. I take a second to appreciate the beauty, somehow connected to my aunt at this moment. She would have loved Ace. I long to tell her how safe he makes me feel, how precious and wanted.

I send my thoughts into the universe, watching the sun slip beneath the mountains.

"Len... Lenny," a slurred voice says from behind me.

I gasp and turn, startled to see Charlie at the other end of the alley. He takes a few steps toward me, stumbling over a wooden pallet before righting himself.

"Um... Charlie, what are you–"

"Where were you last night?" he shouts, his fists balled up at his sides as he stomps closer.

"Last night?" I squeak. *What the heck is going on?*

The man is a few feet from me, and I can smell alcohol on his breath. It's probably seeping through his skin, he's so drunk.

"You deaf? LAST. NIGHT," he bellows. "Where were you?"

I furrow my brow and back away from him, the garbage bags abandoned by my side. "I was out–"

"Yeah, I know you were out," he growls, moving closer to me.

I take another step back, pressing against the brick building. "How did you know?" When he doesn't answer, I try again. "Charlie? How did–"

"CHUCK!" he screams, slamming a hand on the wall right next to my head. I turn away from him, biting my lips to keep from crying. "How many motherfucking times do I have to tell you? Chuck. Chuck. Chuck..." Charlie repeats his name like a demonic chant as he towers over me.

"Okay, okay, Chuck," I say in a soft voice, trying to pacify him.

A sickening smile splits his face, and his eyes are glassy and bloodshot. "That's more like it. I was just looking out for you, babe. You belong to Chuck, not that muscle-headed biker f-fffreak. He's no good for you. He'sss no good for *anyone*."

I clench my jaw and straighten my shoulders, looking this deranged asshole in the eye. "You don't even know him," I state, trying to keep my rising panic at bay. "Ace is a good man. He treats me with more respect than you ever have."

His fist slams down against the wall next to my head, and I squeeze my eyes shut until the vibrations pass. "Ungrateful little... Do you not kn-know anything about the sssstreet rat you ooopened your whore legs for?"

"What?" I yell in his face. I'm shocked at his words, his accusation, and this whole situation.

"Ace isn't even his real name."

"What?" I whisper, blinking a few times.

Charlie's eyes narrow into slits as a sinister grin takes over his features. "Gabe Dekker. He's fifteen years older than you. Got in s-ssome trouble when he was young. His own mother didn't want him. Kicked him to the curb when he was a kid."

"That's awful," I murmur to myself. My heart breaks for my strong, stoic man with hidden pain.

"Not nearly as awful as what he did with his time on the street," Charlie snorts. "Ended up in juvenile detention at fifteen. Got out and headed straight to a biker club. He's their enforcer, Lenny. Do you know what that means?"

I shake my head, unable to form words.

"He beats the living shit out of anyone who pisses the club off. Is that someone you want in your life?"

Tears burn my eyes and clog my throat. It's a lot to take in, but I *know* Ace. He's not the sum of his sins. He's my complicated protector. He's the man who held me on top of a hill while we watched the sunset. He's the man who dressed in a suit and tie because he wanted to impress me. Whatever else he's got going on, we'll figure it out. We have to. We belong together.

"Answer me!" Charlie screams, pounding the wall on either side of my head with his fists.

I try jerking away from him, but Charlie wraps his fingers around my neck and slams me against the wall. A pained whimper leaves my lips as black dots swim in my vision. I claw at his fist, his arm, anywhere I can find purchase.

Charlie snarls like a rabid dog, and I close my eyes, bracing myself for another blow.

It never comes.

Blinking my eyes open, I watch as Charlie is ripped backward, his grip loosening around my neck before he's tossed to the ground.

"Ace," I choke, sliding down the brick wall until I'm curled up in a ball on the ground.

"I'm so sorry, angel," he grits, his deep blue eyes full of rage and regret.

I don't get a chance to say anything before he turns to face Charlie. I bury my face in my hands, knowing my protective biker is taking care of everything. When he's done, I'm going to crawl into his arms and ask him to never let me go again.

Chapter 8

I toss the piece of shit motherfucker on the ground and sink my fist into his face, grunting in satisfaction when I feel his nose snap. Charlie whines like the goddamn weakling he is and curls up on his side. I'm not done with him, however. Not by a long shot.

I grab his collar and pull him off the ground, only to drill my fist into his stomach, sending him flopping back down on the dirty concrete.

"What the hell?" he shrieks, trying to cover his face with his arms.

I wrench them away and grab the dead man by his throat like he did with Lennox. *My* Lennox. This degenerate thought he could lay hands on her, frighten her, threaten her. He thought he could control her with his strength.

Weak motherfucking piece of shit. I'm not a good man by any stretch of the imagination, but my brothers and I still live by a code. No harm to women or children. And the fact that the woman he harmed is mine? That means it's game fucking on.

"How does it feel?" I grit, tightening my grip on his neck. "Having someone stronger than you make you feel helpless?"

His mouth opens and closes like a demonic fish, blood flowing from his broken nose as his wide, panicked eyes plead with me to stop. Charlie makes some strangled sound, attempting to pull my hand away.

"Worthless piece of garbage," I mutter.

I shove him to the ground and land blow after blow to his face, his torso, anywhere I can find purchase. I'm barely aware of roaring motorcycles in the background, but I know it's my brothers. I called them the second I saw Charlie hanging around the alley. I just wish I got here sooner.

Fuck, I hate that my girl had to deal with any of this. Not only did this entitled asshole assault her, but he also painted an all too accurate picture of what a screw-up I am. A homeless, dirty, violent criminal who wasn't wanted by his own mother.

"Ace," someone says from behind me. "Yo, Ace, we got it from here."

I recognize the voice as one of my MC brothers, Diablo, but I growl, continuing to rain down hell on this low-life.

"Ace, back off, man. We got it," Crank adds.

"You want to kill him? He doesn't seem worth it, Ace," Rock says, trying to get through to me.

I'm too far gone now, though. White hot rage permeates every cell as my muscles tense and wind up for more punishment.

"Stop."

I freeze at Lennox's soft-spoken word. So fragile, so broken.

The sound of her voice picks me up and turns me around, carrying me toward her. I have no idea how she's going to react now that she knows the truth of who I am. A monster. A street rat. A hideous blot on society.

I can't look at her, so I stare at the ground. My girl shocks the hell out of me by wrapping her arms around my waist. She buries her head into my chest, sobbing as she clings to me.

"You can't go to jail," she says between sniffles. "You can't leave me."

She doesn't want me to leave her?

I circle my arms around Lennox, pulling her closer. Leaning down, I brush my nose against the top of her head, breathing in her sweet scent. Walking us a few steps backward, I allow Diablo, Crank, and Rock to handle Charlie. He's not dead, but he won't be bothering anyone anytime soon. Good.

Lennox is trembling in my arms, her shoulders heaving up and down with heavy sobs. She's terrified. I pray it's not because of me.

"I'm sorry," I choke, stroking a hand up her spine. "I'm sorry I wasn't here sooner. I'm sorry I'm no good for you. I'm–"

"No good for me?" Lennox breathes, tilting her head back to look me in the eye. "Ace, you saved me. God knows what he would have done if you hadn't..." A shiver runs through her, those golden eyes widening in fear as she realizes how much danger she was in.

Another sob wracks her curvy little body, and I hold her through it. Tucking Lennox into my side, I walk us back inside the coffee shop, stopping briefly to grab her purse and jacket.

"Oh, my god! Lennox, are you okay? What happened?"

"Maribel?" I ask, remembering Lennox mentioning her friend and co-worker. She nods her head, her eyes darting from me to Lennox. "Charlie cornered her out back. He's being taken care of. I'm taking my girl home."

"Of course. Oh, my god, Lennox, I'm so sorry this happened!" Maribel wipes away a few tears and throws her arms around her friend. Lennox hugs her, the two whispering back and forth until Maribel steps back. "Take good care of her," Maribel demands. "You may be a big scary biker, but I think I could take you."

"Maribel," Lennox hisses.

"What?" she stage whispers. "I've got your back."

I nod, my lip twitching with amusement. I'm glad Lennox has a good friend like Maribel. I hope my girl wants me to stick around long enough to meet more of her friends. I don't know how she's going to react to everything that's happened today.

Fifteen minutes later, I pull into my driveway, carefully helping Lennox off my bike before lifting her in my arms.

"I can walk," she murmurs, even as she curls further into my embrace.

I press a kiss to her forehead and continue my journey inside, straight to the bathroom. Setting my sweet girl on the sink counter, I step between her legs, cupping her face in my hands.

"I'm so sorry," I murmur for the tenth time tonight. Running my thumbs over her porcelain cheeks, I take in every inch of her.

"Ace, there's nothing to apologize for," she whispers, bringing her hands up to cover mine. "You saved me. Twice." She tries smiling, but it doesn't reach her eyes.

"But what about…?" I trail off, not knowing how to finish that thought. *What about all the shit you found out about me? What about my hideous past and unforgivable sins?*

"I want to know everything about you," Lennox says, her honeyed voice rolling over me like a balm to my raw, bleeding heart. "But I want to hear it from you."

She drops her hands and leans forward, resting her forehead on mine. I curl my fingers around her hips, anchoring her to me. "It's not a pretty story, angel."

"Tell me anyway. Show me." Lennox slips her hands underneath my shirt, smoothing them over my torso as she drags the material off my body. "Show me who you are, Ace." Her hands find my belt, and she tugs at it, making me suck in a breath.

My girl continues to undress me, then lifts her arms, signaling me to do the same for her. I slowly peel off her shirt, skimming my lips over her shoulders and neck, peppering kisses over her skin as I reveal more and more of it to my hungry eyes.

"Let's shower together," she whispers. "Tell me your story. I'll wash it all away."

Fuck if tears don't burn in the back of my eyes, but I keep them to myself. I don't deserve this angel, but she seems determined to keep me around.

I turn on the water and adjust the temperature before taking Lennox's hand in mine. I guide her into the shower, watching rivulets of water drip down her neck, between her breasts, lower, lower, trickling down her thighs and making me ravenous.

Lennox presses the palms of her hands on my chest, drawing my attention back to her golden eyes. I'm blown away by the understanding I see there. The longing. I can't wrap my head around what she sees in me or why she wants my story, but I'd give this woman anything.

"My ma never wanted me," I say softly. I try looking away from her as shame crawls up my spine, but I can't. Her whiskey-colored eyes draw me in and keep me grounded. "I suppose I didn't give her much reason to keep me around."

I shrug, trying to play it off, but Lennox sees right through me. She kisses my chest and presses her hand over the spot as if to lock it in place. I cover her hand with mine, taking a deep breath before continuing.

"The men she had going in and out of our trailer treated her like shit. When I was big enough to stand up to one of them, I started a fight. Tried throwing the abusive asshole out. I misunderstood the situation, I guess. She took his side. Said I was crazy and a waste of space. I ended up on the curb instead of her useless boyfriend."

"I'm so sorry that happened," Lennox whispers. She grabs a bottle of body wash, pouring some into her hand as she listens to me.

"At thirteen, I had no idea how the world worked. I figured it out real fast, though. No one gave a shit about me, so if I needed something, it was up to me to get it, by any means necessary."

I pause, tilting my head back as Lennox trails her soapy hands over my chest, arms, and torso.

"I stole. Food, cars, clothes. Sold shit on the black market. Finally got picked up by the cops when I was fifteen for dealing pot and squatting in an abandoned building. Spent three years in juvie, then found the Dirty Sinners."

The whole time, Lennox caresses me so gently, tracing the lines of my tattoos and placing sweet kisses over my scars. She's cleaning up my past like she said she would. I gather her hands in mine, kissing her knuckles.

"So you see, I'm not a good man," I rumble, my chest feeling tight and my stomach dropping. "I don't deserve you."

Lennox gives me a radiant smile, one hand coming up to brush my hair out of my eyes.

"I get to decide what I deserve and who I love," she whispers, her cheeks turning the prettiest shade of pink.

"Love?" I echo, my voice caught in my throat.

Lennox nods, nibbling on her bottom lip. "Yeah. I love you, Ace. You may not think you deserve it, but you have it anyway. I love how safe you make me feel, how seen and understood. I love that you're a gruff, growly biker for everyone but me. Only I get to see this side of you, and I'm so honored you want to share yourself with me."

"You love me?" I repeat, still dumbfounded.

"That's what I've been trying to tell you," she says, her hands balling into fists as she rests them on her hips.

A chuckle falls from my lips. I can't believe it. This gorgeous, brilliant, sweet, kind, sexy as hell woman loves me. She's so fucking adorable, especially when she's all wound up. I know exactly how I want to celebrate this moment.

"I love you so fucking much," I growl before claiming her lips.

Lennox gasps as I pull her against me, letting her feel my need. She moans and grinds against me as I slip my tongue past her lips, tangling it with hers.

"Gonna show you how much, beautiful. Are you ready for that?"

"Yes, please."

Chapter 9

Lennox

I feel the weight of his gaze all over my body as he takes in every naked inch. "Fucking gorgeous," he murmurs. Ace runs the back of his knuckles over my breasts, my pebbled nipples, and down my ribcage until they land on my hips.

I gasp as he grips me tightly and presses me into his chiseled body so I can feel his hard cock against my stomach. He takes my lips then, in a slow, drugging kiss. My hands wind around the back of his head, and I pull him even closer.

"I need inside of you, baby girl," he groans.

I giggle at his seemingly desperate need and then moan when he pushes me up against the wall and grips my ass, rolling my hips into his erection. His fingers tease my entrance and then glide up my slit, checking my readiness.

"So goddamn wet for me. Gonna fuck you now," he growls.

With that, he lifts me in his arms and pins me to the wall, his thick dick hitting home inside my throbbing cunt. He fucks me hard and fast, grunting with each thrust of his hips. I lean forward and bite his lips before kissing him wildly. I didn't realize how much I needed him like this, needed to feel him deep inside me again.

"Yes, Ace. God, don't stop," I moan.

He's relentless as he pounds into me, nailing me to the wall with each rough stroke, breaking me apart so perfectly. I feel every ridge of his cock as it splits me open and glides along my tight channel. My fingernails bite into the flesh on his shoulders, making him roar and fuck me harder.

My orgasm slams into me by surprise, knocking the air out of my lungs as I convulse in his arms and open my mouth in a silent scream. Fire rips through my veins, leaving every nerve raw and exposed.

Before I even have the chance to come down, Ace pulls out of me and sets me down on the ground, spinning me around so I have to brace myself on the wall with my ass sticking out toward him.

"Fuck, yes, so perfect. So thick and juicy and *mine*," he growls before sliding into me from behind.

Ace is almost gentle, teasing me, rubbing my clit, building me up touch by touch. His hot breath rolls against my neck as his hands tighten around my hips, keeping a slow, steady rhythm.

I moan and buck against him when his hands slide up my hips, following the curve of my waist until they cup my breasts. I gasp when he pinches my nipples. Reaching one hand up, I grab his hair as he kisses me over my shoulder.

I run my hand down his cheek and cup it there, his coarse stubble rubbing the palm of my hand. He works his cock in and out, deeper, deeper, so fucking deep, grinding into me and sparking a desperate need to come again. My body burns for release, my skin scorching, my lungs breathing fire.

"Don't stop," I plead, rocking back and meeting him thrust for thrust.

"Never," he growls, picking up speed.

Our skin slaps together as he builds us up with every stroke of his fat cock. Ace curls his body over mine and places his hands on either side of mine against the shower wall. I feel his muscles bunch and tense against my back and ass. Something about that makes my pussy clench and gush.

"Oh, God, Ace, I'm... I'm..."

"Let go, love. Let go of every-fucking-thing and come for me."

I hold my breath as every muscle stretches tight against my skin. All at once, every ounce of tension is released from my body as my pussy spasms around him again and again. Ace pistons in and out of me, keeping me at my peak longer than I've ever experienced. I cry and sob and beg for mercy as sharp pleasure bordering on pain stabs at my nerves and prickles over my skin.

Ace unleashes a torrent of cum deep inside me. It splashes down my legs, mixing with my juices from multiple orgasms.

"Christ, baby, I'm coming so fucking hard," he grunts as his cock jerks inside me and empties another round of his release.

Ace pulls out of me and spins me around, guiding me to lean against the wall as he kneels before me.

"Oh, my God, Ace, I can't..."

He just growls and lifts my right leg over his shoulder before licking up our combined juices. God, it's so hot how he drinks down our releases like a feral animal. When his tongue swipes against my clit, my body twitches so hard he has to grip my hips to keep me steady. He never lets up, though.

Ace sucks my clit with such a singular intensity I start to feel lightheaded and tingly all over. He growls into my throbbing, raw pussy, and nibbles at my clit, causing a great pull deep in my belly. Again and again, he lavishes attention on my swollen ball of nerves until I come violently against his mouth.

He holds me through it, catching me when I collapse into his arms. Ace nuzzles into the side of my neck, still breathing heavily as he whispers how beautiful and perfect I am.

We eventually untangle ourselves and dry off, but Ace doesn't let me get very far. He scoops me up in his arms and carries me across the hall into his room. I giggle as he tosses me onto the bed, then moan when he crawls over me, dragging his lips up my neck until he's nibbling on my ear.

"Love that sound, beautiful," he murmurs, making me smile.

Ace rolls over, draping me across his chest before pulling the blankets over our naked bodies. I snuggle up against my warm, cuddly, sexy-as-hell biker, resting my head on his chest. He runs his fingers up and down my spine in calming strokes while I listen to the steady beat of his heart.

"What are you thinking about?" I whisper.

Ace pauses his soft touch, taking a deep breath before his fingers resume their path along my back. "I still can't believe you want me," he answers, his words almost inaudible.

I prop myself up on his chest, looking him in the eyes. Dark blue irises stare back at me, a million little silver specs revealing his true emotions. My man has been through hell and back, and it's going to take more than a few days for him to trust I'm not going anywhere. "Are you scared?"

"Only that I'm going to mess it up somehow."

I lean forward, resting my forehead on his. "Would you ever leave me?"

"No," comes his instant, emphatic response.

I grin and kiss the tip of his nose. "Good. All those feelings you have for me? I have them for you, too. I'm not leaving you, Ace. I love you."

Ace closes his eyes, breathing in deeply. When he opens them again, I see the hint of tears, though he blinks them away in the next second. God, I love him so much. It kills me that he spent so many years feeling like garbage. Never again.

"I love you so much, Lennox. I've never... It's like... I want... fuck it, I'm no good at words," he says with a sigh.

"It's okay. Just tell me what you can," I say gently, brushing some hair out of his face.

Ace gathers up my fingers and kisses each one. "I need to claim you."

He's so freaking sweet to me, and I don't think he's even aware of it. "I think you've done that plenty, but I'm up for another round..."

Ace's eyes turn dark, and he smirks, making me feel all sorts of things. I may need to jump his bones sooner rather than later. "While I definitely want to do that, too, I meant I need to claim you in front of my brothers. At the clubhouse."

"Uh, what? You mean they all watch us...?" My face burns bright red at the thought.

"Hell, no," Ace snarls. "Not like that. Jesus, if anyone ever saw you naked..." He wipes a hand down his face, and I lean forward, kissing him on the cheek. I love how possessive he is. "You'll have a leather cut similar to mine, and I'll announce in front of my brothers that you're my woman and I'm your man."

"Special clothes, a speech in front of friends... sounds almost like a wedding." I clap my hand over my mouth as soon as the words are spoken. *Am I really already talking about marriage?*

Ace's features turn serious, his gaze sharp as he stares through me. I open my mouth to take it back, but he lunges forward, wrapping his fingers in my hair and tilting my head back. I moan into his kiss, welcoming the rough strokes of his tongue against mine like he can't get enough.

"Fuck, yes. I want you to be mine in every way. My old lady, my wife, the mother of my children. Everything. I want it all, Lennox."

"Ace," I whisper, tears gathering behind my eyes. I have no words, so I nod, hoping he knows that's exactly what I want, too.

"I've got you," he murmurs, tucking my head under his chin. Ace combs his fingers through my hair and trails them down my spine before reversing his path.

I snuggle closer, my heart completely full. I'm no longer alone, waiting for my life to start. Breathing in Ace's earthy scent, feeling the heat of his skin, his tender touch on my back... I know I've found my happily ever after with the most perfect man in the world.

Epilogue

Ace

"Happy birthday, dear Callie, happy birthday to you!"

My little girl laughs and claps her hands before blowing out the candles on her cake. She looks over her shoulder at me, her eyes the same golden color as her mother's. I wink at her while Lennox proceeds to cut the cake and hand the pieces out to the other kids.

It's hard to believe Callie is three today. I remember holding her little body in my arms when she was born and realizing my heart had a bigger capacity for love than I could have ever dreamed. It's all thanks to my incredible wife.

Lennox somehow knows I'm thinking about her. She peers up at me from across the table, giving me a radiant smile. I tip my head back and to the side, indicating she should follow me out into the hall.

A few seconds later, my gorgeous wife is by my side. I drag her out of the dining room, spinning her around so her back is pressed against the wall. Leaning forward, I cover her body with mine, pinning her in place with my hands anchored at her hips.

Lennox gives me a wicked smile, one I have to taste. I claim her lips, coaxing her mouth to part as I slide my tongue inside. My woman melts against me, her body pliant as I squeeze and mold her flesh in my massive hands.

"What was that for?" she pants when she finally breaks the kiss. Lennox rests her head against the wall while I nuzzle into the side of her neck.

"I saw you there, all pretty and tempting as fuck," I murmur, my voice three octaves lower than normal.

"Ace, it's our daughter's birthday party," Lennox hisses, though she has a hint of a smirk on her lips.

"All the more reason to celebrate," I grunt, nipping at her skin. I love the way it makes her squirm against me.

She laughs and presses her palms against my chest, pushing me back slightly. I frown, but my girl just rolls her eyes. I love seeing her playful, sassy side and how confident she's become in the last few years.

Lennox gets up on her tiptoes and kisses my cheek before spinning away and waltzing back into the dining room. I hang back for a few moments, not wanting to go into a room full of kids while I'm ravenous for my wife.

Walking into the kitchen, I fill a glass with water and slam it down. It's not until I turn around to put the glass in the dishwasher that I realize I'm not alone.

"Hey, Leif." I greet the ex-Marine with a tip of my chin, then ask if he wants a beer.

He shakes his head, his eyes darting to the dining room where Maribel is celebrating with the other kids and parents.

"Needed some space?" I ask.

He nods.

"Take your time. You know where everything is. Want me to send Maribel in if I see her?"

The tall, muscled tank of a man with dark hair and darker eyes gets the dopiest look on his face. "I'd never say no to that."

I chuckle and clap him on the shoulder as I head out of the kitchen. Leif and Maribel have been together for a while now, but he's still not used to being in crowds, especially noisy ones. He's done a lot of work on himself lately, but I know he's still haunted and traumatized by his time in the military.

I'm not sure how Maribel finally broke through to him, but the two have a special connection. I'd never have believed it in a million years if I hadn't experienced something similar myself.

Leaning against the back wall, I watch Callie laugh with her friends while getting frosting all over her face. Lennox comes around the corner, and I loop my arm around her waist, pulling her back against my chest.

She gasps, then relaxes when she sees it's me. "Hey," she whispers, tipping her head back to rest against my shoulder.

I hold her against me, spreading a hand over her stomach while kissing her temple. "Hey, angel."

Lennox sighs contentedly, letting me gently rock her back and forth. We watch our daughter make an absolute mess of her cake, loving every minute.

I never thought my life would turn out like this, but now I can't picture it any other way. I have the most perfect, gorgeous, kind woman as my partner, and we created the cutest little girl on the planet. I still struggle to believe I deserve any of this, but Lennox is always here to remind me I'm worthy of love.

She took a few years off from the coffee shop after Callie was born, but she started back part-time a few months ago. Instead of making coffee and running the register, my incredible wife struck a deal with the owner. She goes in four mornings a week and bakes up a storm, stocking the bakery case full to bursting. She gets paid hourly as well as a percentage of each bakery sale.

Like I said, she's amazing. Beautiful, smart, and the sweetest woman I've ever met.

"I love my life with you," I whisper into the shell of her ear.

She looks at me over her shoulder, those golden eyes sparkling with all the love in the world. I can't breathe when all of her attention is directed at me. "I love every day with you, Ace."

"Me too, baby."

Lennox settles back against me, and I hold her close, soaking up everything about this moment. Never thought I wanted a family. Never thought I deserved one. But this right here? This is perfect. If Lennox thinks I'm worthy of love, there must be something redeemable about this dirty sinner.

Connect with me!

Check out my website, cameronhart.net[1], for sneak previews on my latest projects.

Follow me on social media:

Facebook Page - facebook.com/cameronhartauthor
    Instagram - instagram.com/cameron.hart.author
    TikTok - tiktok.com/@author.cameron.hart
    Goodreads - goodreads.com/16081533.Cameron_Hart
    Bookbub - bookbub.com/authors/cameron-hart

---

1. https://cameronhart.net/

Also by Cameron Hart

Check out my other popular series and books!
Mafia, MC, & Bodyguard Romance:
<u>Moscatelli Crime Family Series</u>[2]
<u>Di Salvo Crime Family Series</u>[3]
<u>Chaos MC series</u>[4]
<u>Savage Ride</u>[5]
Mountain Man Romance:
<u>Men of Blackthorne Mountain Series</u>[6]
<u>Bear's Tooth Mountain Men Series</u>[7]
Cowboy & Small Town Romance:
<u>Roped in by Love Series</u>[8]

---

2. https://books2read.com/u/mqBaze

3. https://books2read.com/u/m0odzW

4. https://books2read.com/u/bMVAOk

5. https://books2read.com/u/bMVlG7

6. https://books2read.com/u/3RYDvB

7. https://books2read.com/u/mVel7A

8. https://books2read.com/u/3RYlBY